PRAISE FOR CARY HERWIG AND THE ARMY BRAT HAUNTINGS

"Friends Like Dust is a paranormal page-turner that will haunt you to the last page."

— PAMELA K. KINNEY, AUTHOR
OF *WEREWOLVES, DOGMEN, AND OTHER
SHAPESHIFTERS* AND THE YA FANTASY *DEMON
MEMORIES*

"Cary Herwig's *The World Ends at the River* perfectly captures the languid summer days in the South of the 1950s. You feel the sticky heat, hear the drone of bees, see the lightning bugs at night . . . and you also feel deeply for the protagonist, a young girl on the verge of womanhood who discovers her family's unearthly inheritance and the consequences that it brings. I kept turning page after page . . . and I will be waiting eagerly for the next installment. Highly recommended."

— KATHRYN PTACEK, AUTHOR OF
SHADOWEYES AND EDITOR OF *WOMEN OF
DARKNESS*

"*The Ghost's Daughter* by Cary Herwig is a suspense-filled novel that held my attention throughout. This novel took me back to the 1950s when society expected women to be seen and not heard . . . I loved Vivien's courage and dedication to her family. Thank you for this captivating story."

—JENNIFER IBIAM, *READERS' FAVORITE*

FRIENDS LIKE DUST

FRIENDS LIKE DUST

THE ARMY BRAT HAUNTINGS
BOOK THREE

CARY HERWIG

November 1957, Asnières-la-Giraud, France

Vivien settled into the big, overstuffed chair and opened the book. It was midafternoon on Friday after Thanksgiving and there was no school, so she'd finished reading H.G. Wells's *The Invisible Man* and started *The Knight of Maison Rouge* by Dumas. On Thanksgiving Day, they'd all gone into Fontenet and had a huge dinner in the mess hall on post, along with a dozen or more other families.

Turkey and dressing and all the trimmings, pies, fresh oranges and apples, seen only at this time of year, and nuts in the shell. They ate until they knew they would burst. And leftovers? They brought home a whole turkey and bowls of the sides, an apple pie and a pumpkin pie, a bag of fruit, and another of nuts. Anything left went to people in the village of Fontenet to be distributed to the poor. Why had they prepared so much more food than needed?

Mama spent late afternoon cutting up the turkey and boiling the carcass to make stock. Still feeling full when suppertime came, they each settled for another slice of pie. Today, Friday, Daddy had the duty, meaning he would be at headquarters from noon until next morning.

Vivien found her place in the book and immersed herself in the world of The Terror, what some called the French revolution. A few minutes later, someone knocked on the door. Vivien looked up, resenting the interruption. They didn't expect anyone. As usual, they didn't live in post housing, making them distant from most of the other families. She'd made few friends at school. She always found it hard to relate to other kids and, to be honest, she didn't mind.

She placed her bookmark between the pages and closed the book. At the door from the living room into the hall, she stopped to listen.

Mama gently told whoever knocked on the door to go away. The person—a woman by the voice—spoke in an odd language. Vivien picked up the card from the top of the record player and handed it to Mama. Printed in French and English, it said, "We are Americans and do not speak French. We cannot buy what you are selling. Thank you. Goodbye."

Mama handed the card to the woman standing on the high stoop. Vivien, puzzled by the woman's appearance, soon realized the woman must be a Gypsy, the first she'd ever seen.

The Gypsy woman smiled, showing gaps in her teeth. Large, gold, hoop earrings swayed when she nodded to Mama and handed back the card. She wore wool gloves and carried a square basket in one hand, probably filled with whatever she wanted to sell. A heavy, wool shawl with gold thread reflecting the light wrapped around her stooped shoulders, and a colorful head scarf had been tied under her chin. She looked exactly how movies and TV shows would portray an old Gypsy woman.

She kept talking; however, it didn't sound like French. She leaned around Mama to look at Vivien, standing three feet behind, and stopped speaking. Her eyes grew wide, and she cocked her head to one side and stared. Before either of them could stop her, the woman stepped around Mama and came to Vivien. She took Vivien's hands in both of hers. They felt dry, like old paper, all brown and wrinkled. She turned Vivien's hands over and looked at the palms.

Again, she spoke in the strange language. Mama looked alarmed and reached to grab the woman's arm.

"No, Mama. It's all right."

The woman let go and looked from her to Mama, made a little curtsey and went to the door. She said something more, and Vivien had the impression she spoke of something other than selling whatever the trinkets might be in her small basket.

The woman stepped out onto the stoop and disappeared down the steep, concrete steps toward the back of the house. Mama shut the door, and Vivien raced to the large window in the kitchen. The woman crossed the back yard and pushed the fence away from the corner of the shed. She edged through the opening and walked up the hill, toward a group of caravans.

"What on earth was that all about?" Mama asked.

Vivien exhaled. "She saw something when she looked at me."

"What?"

"Can Gypsies really tell fortunes and know about a person's past?"

"I didn't think so."

Vivien returned to the living room and plopped down in

the overstuffed chair, her favorite place to read. She picked up the book but didn't open it. Mama went into the kitchen, where she'd been cutting up vegetables and turkey for soup. Vivien's younger sister, Lauren, appeared from the bedroom and asked Mama who had knocked on the door. Mama explained, stressing the importance of not letting anyone they didn't know into the house.

Vivien tried to read. When the old woman looked so intently at her, she'd felt an understanding pass between them. Of what? Of seeing ghosts and wanting to help them? Maybe. She felt a tingling in her hands when the woman held hers, almost like an electric shock, but gentler. It ran through her body, and she'd wanted to laugh. The connection didn't last.

Twilight came and they ate. They turned on lights and cleaned up the kitchen.

Vivien had returned to reading when someone knocked on the door again. The three of them looked at each other. "It's her," Vivien said and went to the door herself this time. The woman held out her hands, palms up, and Vivien placed her own against them, feeling the same tingling as before. The woman turned Vivien's hands and looked at her palms again. Vivien looked up from the touch of the smaller, browner hands into the very dark eyes.

"How do . . ."

The woman appeared to glow against the near darkness. She smiled slightly and curtsied. While making some sort of sign with her left hand aimed toward Vivien, she murmured what might be either a curse or a blessing. Vivien closed her eyes and lowered her head. When she looked up, the woman held out a small cloth bag tied with a drawstring.

"I can't . . ."

The woman shook her head. "Gift."

"For me?"

"Yours."

Vivien took it. The woman made another hand sign, curtsied again, and disappeared into the night. Mama stepped out onto the stoop and looked toward the back yard.

"She's gone." She followed Vivien into the kitchen. They both sat at the table.

"What's in the bag?" Lauren looked frightened while she watched Vivien open the small bag and turn it upside down.

A pendant on a black silk cord dropped into her hand. It felt cold and, instinctively, she closed her hand to warm it. About an inch and a half long, the pendant consisted of two stones, one wrapped in a gold-colored metal. It sat above a black stone, about half the total length, longer than it was wide, with six sides and ending in a sharp point. The top stone, round and nearly white with rainbow colors shifting through it, had been set in a gold-colored metal. The surround came to a point at both bottom and top. The top point had been pierced so the silk cord could run through it.

Vivien held it up by the cord so that the stones reflected the light. Lauren came closer and reached toward it without touching it. Vivien lowered it gently to the kitchen table.

"What are the stones, Mama?"

"I'm not sure. The top one looks like opal. The black one could be onyx." She picked it up and balanced the pendant in her hand. "It's heavy enough to be real gold, but that may be the weight of the stones." She laid it back down. "It may be a talisman or an amulet to protect you."

"Because of the ghosts?"

"Maybe. Who knows? It smacks of witchcraft, though."

Sudden fear made Vivien ask, "I can keep it, can't I?"

Mama looked from the pendant to her daughter. Vivien's own fear reflected from her mother's eyes.

"We'll see. Maybe a book in the library on talismans can tell us what this one is supposed to be for. Don't wear it for a while."

Vivien couldn't promise.

O n Saturday, Mama and the girls drove to the post to do the shopping and visit the library. They left Daddy at home, still sleeping after the long hours of duty on Friday.

Although Mama had been nervous about qualifying for the international driver's license she needed to drive on French roads, she came through with flying colors. Most of her driving time consisted of these Saturday outings.

They'd shipped the old Chevy over, and she didn't have to learn to drive a new car on top of learning new rules. The speedometer registered miles-per-hour, while the speed limit signs were in kilometers-per-hour. She had trouble converting the numbers, so she always drove slowly and carefully.

First, they went to the snack bar and next to the PX, or post exchange, to get the Sunday papers. They always got at least three so Mama and Daddy could keep up with what went on back in the States and the girls could read the comics. Vivien tackled the Sunday crossword puzzle each week but never finished more than a third of one. Solving puzzles, reading the papers, and reading library books took the place of watching television. The area had no American or English TV stations, even if they had a set to watch it on.

Next, they visited the post library housed in the USO building. They had a surprising number of books. Between it and the school library, the two girls had plenty to read.

This time, Mama went in too, looking for books on semi-precious stones and talismans. She found two. The girls still searched the shelves for more books to check out, so Mama left the two she found with Vivien and went on to the commissary to do the grocery shopping.

Selecting foods had turned into a new adventure. Strange brands replaced those familiar back home. Some things they could get on the French market. However, they'd been warned not to consume things like milk or fresh vegetables and fruits, which, according to the Army, weren't safe. The milk because French farmers didn't vaccinate their cows against tuberculosis. Fresh produce because the farmers used human waste to fertilize their fields. They'd already seen what Americans called "honey buckets," small containers similar to gasoline haulers, in fields being pulled by tractors spreading its contents over the ground.

The girls finished their book selection and waited outside on a bench. The weather had been cold since they arrived in France in October, definitely colder than in Tennessee. Vivien enjoyed the crisp cold air since it gave her the chance to wear her new coat. Lauren, not so much, new coat or not.

Soon, Mama pulled up, and they got in the car and headed home. They stopped at the gate in the low wall around the house. Vivien got out and opened it, then closed it after Mama pulled the car in. Daddy still slept, so the three of them carried everything in, while trying to be quiet.

They'd become used to the house pretty quickly. High ceilings in the four rooms, each large squares: two bedrooms, a living room that must also have been used as a dining room by the earlier tenants, and a kitchen, where they ate most of their meals. A large dining table had been pushed into a corner of the living room, used mostly for storage of library books, the newspapers, and anything they couldn't put elsewhere. The girls studied there, too.

Closets didn't exist, and a large wardrobe stood in the master bedroom. The girls hung their clothes in a makeshift wardrobe of plywood on three sides, with a rod nailed across and a curtain hanging in front.

Both rooms had a large chest of drawers, and Mama had an old steamer trunk sitting open in one corner of their room for storing her underwear, handkerchiefs, and other personal items. She found it in a store in St.-Jean-d'Angély, the largest town close to Fontenet. The former tenants, another Army family, left behind a sofa and the overstuffed chair. They picked up other pieces from families moving back to the States. They still needed odds and ends, like a coffee table and bedside tables.

The bathroom took some getting used to. The same width as the hall, it had a small hot water heater hanging on the wall. They'd grown accustomed to Saturday night baths in Tennessee. Here everyone could enjoy the luxury of a shower twice a week, just on different days. The rest of the time, they washed up each morning before going out. Mama called it a whore bath. Vivien found that funny while Lauren didn't understand it. Because hot water was at a premium, they heated water for washing dishes on the stove in the kitchen.

For heat, a large oil heater sat in the hallway. They put a chair next to it so the girls could dress near the heat in the cold mornings. Mama did a lot of baking, and the oven warmed the kitchen. At night, they burned wood in the fireplaces, one in the living room and one in each bedroom. Small and built into the corner of each room, the surrounds and mantels were made of purple marble. Daddy scrounged wood on post, but they'd have to find a better source. The house never really warmed up, like the bedroom in Grandma's house.

Mama checked the heater in the hall, then went into the bedroom to waken Daddy. They could be heard murmuring as the girls moved around putting things away. Vivien turned on the radio, a large wooden console with record player on the top under a hinged cover, also left behind by a previous tenant. American soldiers had been renting the house for several years. Daddy said living on the "economy" cost less than living in post housing. The girls felt disappointed in not having the amenities they'd hoped for after living with an outhouse and lack of heat for a year, things like a warm house, running hot water and a bathtub. When they moved from one place to another, the Army allowed only so much in household goods by weight. The radio weighed a lot and probably would never be taken to the States.

It took a moment for the radio to warm up. The station they listened to broadcast out of England and played much of the latest American rock and roll music. At the moment, Buddy Holly sang "Peggy Sue," one of Vivien's favorites. She much preferred him to Elvis.

Daddy came into the living room and kissed Vivien on the top of her head. "Where's Lauren?"

"In the bedroom, looking through her books."

He nodded and went into the kitchen. Mama fixed him breakfast, and when he finished eating, he went outside to work on the car. Vivien followed. While he worked, she handed him the tools he asked for. She preferred this to helping Mama clean the house or do the laundry. At least the wet clothes didn't have to be hung outside. One of the earlier tenants had strung a line in the basement. It was still cold down there, but without a wind, which made hanging out the laundry so much worse.

Later that night, Mama and Vivien sat at the kitchen table looking through the books on crystals and talismans. "I think that whitish stone might be tourmaline instead of opal." Mama showed Vivien the pictures in the book. "Or it might be some sort of moonstone. It's difficult to tell. They all have some sort of protective powers. If you believe in that sort of thing."

"Well, we believe in ghosts," Vivien said.

Mama smiled and nodded. "We do indeed."

ON MONDAY MORNING, the girls quickly dressed by the oil stove. Their school bus came early, before the sun peeked above the horizon. They hadn't gotten used to getting up so early. Vivien gathered up her books and notebook and set them on the large living room table. The kitchen table had been set for breakfast. Vivien sat down and tried to look through the window for the Gypsy camp on the hill. The light shining through the high kitchen window reflected back from fog, hiding the world outside.

Lauren came in and Mama spooned out hot oatmeal. Vivien added a glob of butter and two spoons of sugar. She spooned oatmeal onto a slice of buttered toast. They ate quickly so they would be ready for the bus when it came.

Daddy had to be on duty at five. He got breakfast on post, so Mama didn't have to get up even earlier. The bus picked the girls up first on their route at 6:30. Most of their ride in the small Renault bus each morning was in the dark.

The bus's headlights barely pierced the fog, and the French driver took it slowly. He knew the route well, although the narrow roads through the rural area could be full of surprises. Once, a brown cow stood in the middle of the road, its eyes eerily reflecting the headlights. PFC Harris, the bus guard, got out and chased the cow into a field as if he'd done it before.

He kept an eye out for anything that might cause trouble. The "mox nix stick" waved up and down, the light at the end blinked to signal their turns. Everyone found these turn signals very funny, like nothing they'd seen back home, and everyone called it by that name, meaning "maybe the vehicle would turn, maybe not." Surprisingly, most all French drivers signaled turns and lane changes.

Five students rode the bus each morning, half of what it could hold. By the time the bus picked up the last one, the sky lightened in the east. When they pulled into the parking area at the school, daylight had come.

One other bus had arrived just minutes before they did. They couldn't get into the buildings until the bell rang. To amuse themselves and keep warm, some of the students played tag.

More buses arrived, the bell finally rang, and Vivien watched to be sure Lauren headed toward the second building and her fourth-grade class. With a small number of students in each class, the teachers each taught two grades. Vivien, in the seventh grade, joined her classmates and those in the eighth grade in the classroom in the main building. It also housed the principal's office and the library. Mr. Gregerson, both principal and teacher for the seventh and eighth grades, shared the office with the school secretary, Madame Guilbeau, who also taught everyone French.

Most of the kids made fun of Madame Guilbeau, who seemed such a sour person. She rarely smiled, and when she did, it didn't improve that hatchet face of hers. Her chin and nose were long and pointed, resembling the witch in *The Wizard of Oz* movie.

Vivien kept her coat on. It took a while for the heat to warm the room, since the furnace was turned way down at night and on weekends. If it got warm enough, she would hang the coat on one of the hooks in the hall.

Everyone talked and laughed. She hadn't connected with anyone and wondered if she would. The eighth graders had no interest in younger kids, and the two other girls in the seventh grade were fast friends. One of the drawbacks of living outside of the military housing, she and Lauren didn't get to interact with the others except at school. Lauren made friends much faster and already had a girl to pal around with.

Every student had to take either art or music, and in the afternoon, Vivien went to the third building where Miss Lawrence taught music. It was a break from her own classroom where Mr. Gregersen taught seventh- and eighth-grade math, science, history, English, and social studies. This afternoon, Vivien sat outside during recess reading *The Good Shepherd*, about a Navy ship in the North Atlantic during World War II. She'd become interested in the subject after sailing on the *Randall*, or the *U.S.S. General George M. Randall*, to be precise. The post library had quite a few works of World War II fiction, and she had checked out three the last time.

She stopped reading and looked around the playground, feeling that someone watched her. None of the other kids paid her any attention. No strangers or possible ghosts lurked in the yard. The fog thinned enough for her to see a few yards beyond the fence. Nothing there. She breathed a sigh of relief. Life had become strange enough without a ghost to contend with. If it was going to happen, let it be next summer when life in their new home had become more familiar. Not now.

The bus ride home reversed the morning route, and they

were first to get home in the afternoon. Through the swirls of light fog behind the house, Vivien saw the Gypsies' camp on the hill. Mama said with temperatures falling they probably would move to warmer climes. Vivien wanted to visit the camp and learn more about the pendant. Maybe find out what the old woman thought might happen in the future.

She looked at the clock on the kitchen wall. Daddy got home at five, so she had an hour. "Mama, I'm going outside for a while."

"All right. Don't go far."

THREE

The wire fence, once attached to the corner of the shed in the northeast corner of the back yard, had come loose at some point. It could easily be pushed far enough to slip through, as demonstrated by the Gypsy woman.

Vivien looked up at the kitchen window to make sure Mama didn't see her when she pushed the edge of the fence away from the shed and squeezed through. The field going up the hill looked smoother than it was. Dirt clods from plowing made the ground uneven. Some sort of grass hid them, possibly winter wheat. Vivien had heard of such a planting but had no idea what it might look like.

Until now, she'd only seen the wagons from a distance, too far to make out the bright colors and designs. Five of them formed a circle, two still hooked up to the old cars that pulled them from place to place. A pickup and two more cars sat outside of the circle. Smoke rose in a column from a fire in the center. Voices came to her as she got closer. Children chased each other around the wagons. One stopped on seeing her and watched a moment. She ran to one of the wagons, calling out to someone.

Vivien entered the circle. All voices quieted. A man rose from the steps of a wagon and started toward her. The old woman stepped out of another wagon. "Paolo." She spoke to him, but Vivien couldn't understand the words. He nodded and went back to sit on the steps.

Vivien walked to the woman, who stood looking at her curiously. She no longer stooped, standing straight and taller than she'd first appeared, although a few inches shorter than Vivien. The head scarf was gone, revealing auburn hair twisted into a bun at the nape of her neck.

"You've come sooner than I expected," the woman said with a strong accent.

"You speak English."

"I speak many languages. Some well. Some not so much." She motioned for Vivien to sit in a lawn chair near her wagon. "What do you want?"

Cooking odors wafted to her as the breeze shifted. Something smelled good and Vivien's mouth watered.

"I'm not sure. Well, the pendant you gave me." She took it out of the pocket of her coat.

"It is a protection amulet. You have a . . . a talent which presents certain dangers for you."

"I see ghosts."

"I know." The woman held out her hand, and Vivien lay the pendant in her palm. "These stones will provide protection. Still, you must also be careful."

"Careful of what?"

"Not all ghosts are friendly."

Vivien thought of Nurse Armstrong who wanted to keep her, thinking she was her lost child, scaring her with a vision of a dark jungle. Of Yoshi Narita who drowned in the ford and wanted to prove Mr. McCarthy wasn't her murderer. The woman ghost on the ship who tried to protect her and Lauren from the angry ghost of the young soldier who stole life energy from children.

"You were born to see ghosts. Your mother also saw ghosts at your age. The ghosts you see are more dangerous, I think. Whether it's because of the time you live in . . ." She shrugged.

"Will I see one here?"

"There are many restless spirits. There are many ways in which a ghost can be dangerous to you."

"I don't understand."

"You care too much. You wish to help too much. Never lose connection to your family."

"What . . ."

"That is all I have seen. All I know. Yours is a gift, but it is also a curse."

Vivien wondered if any of this helped. She had been afraid with each ghostly experience. Now, the woman made her more afraid.

"Can I lose this . . . this . . ."

"Unlike your mother and her mother before her, your gift will not fade as quickly. It may be gone one day."

A great weight settled on Vivien's shoulders. Believing once she grew up, she would see no more ghosts had made it all seem bearable.

The woman leaned toward her and handed back the amulet. "Wear this, especially in the presence of a ghost. It will weaken their hold on you."

"Thank you."

They rose and before Vivien could turn away, the woman came close and hugged her. Without another word, she climbed into her wagon. Vivien looked down the hill at the house where Mama would be putting dinner on the table. Dusk had fallen, and the kitchen light shone through the window, guiding her home.

FOUR

Tuesday night, they all went to the newly opened Christmas store on post. Daddy picked out a live tree and two strings of lights. They found a variety of tree ornaments different from those they had used for many years. Mama and the girls each picked out a box. They got lots of tinsel. As a treat, they ate hamburgers at the snack bar before heading home.

It took all four of them to carry the large dining table to the living room window. The live tree was planted in a large bucket. Daddy set it on top of several layers of newspaper to keep water from ruining the table. Mama wrapped an old bed sheet around the bucket to hide it. Sitting atop the table, the whole tree could be seen though the tall French windows facing the main street of the village. They all had their part: Daddy put on the lights and supervised, making sure all sides of the tree were decorated. Mama hung the first ornaments. The girls hung the remaining ornaments and looped tinsel over branches a few strands at a time. Soon, lights shone red, green, blue, and white. Ornaments reflected their colors, and the ceiling light made the tinsel sparkle where it dangled from the branches.

For the next several nights, people of the village walked past the house to look at the tree. They would stand near the gate, pointing toward the window and smile. Parents lifted their children so they could get a good look over the gate.

Vivien and Lauren thought it very sad French people didn't put up Christmas trees in their homes, but when they went into St. Jean to shop, they found decorated trees lining the main street. Each one had been tied against the corner of a building with a few lights and other decorations on the sides facing out. They looked bare compared to their own tree, yet pretty at the same time.

They went into the large department store to buy presents. Vivien loved buying presents and spent much of her allowance she'd saved on gifts for everyone in the family. She got Lauren a diary with the dates printed in French. For Mama, she found pretty writing paper. Daddy was the hard one to buy for. She settled on a small cigarette lighter. He didn't smoke a lot, and she felt a guilty about buying it, always hoping Daddy would quit.

Mama had bought paper and ribbon at the holiday store on post, and as soon as she could, Vivien shut herself in the bedroom and covered the bed with paper, ribbons, boxes, and gifts. Every gift had to be wrapped just right. It took more than an hour for her to finish. She loved using lots of different paper, so the packages looked colorful and festive. She curled and twisted ribbon into bows to tape on top.

On the Friday before Christmas, a stack of brightly wrapped packages lay under the tree. Mama had found a garland of paper rings among the things they'd brought from the States and hung it across the window. It all looked bright and cheerful, good for the grey and dull days leading to the holiday and days off from school.

Mama announced a change in their usual holiday plans. She had pushed two packages under the tree to one side. She and Lauren usually got to open one present on Christmas Eve. This time it would be earlier.

Puzzled, Vivien opened the large package with her usual care. Don't rip the paper. Save both paper and bow. Lauren tore into hers and got it open sooner. Mama and Daddy hovered, watching. There must be something special about these presents. Vivien threw caution to the winds and tore off the paper.

Lauren held hers up first: a new dress fit for a party, with red and green plaid skirt and green velvet bodice. In the box, under the dress, she found her first crinoline slip. "Oh, thank you, thank you. They're beautiful. Can I—"

"Go try it on," Mama said.

Meanwhile, Vivien folded the tissue paper aside. She could feel Mama's eyes watching her while she lifted up her own new dress. Unfolding it, first she saw the white bodice with three-quarter length sleeves. Red ribbon trimmed the jewel neckline and edges of the sleeves. She stood and raised it higher. The solid red, full skirt opened out. It was the most beautiful dress she'd ever seen.

"Do you like it?"

"Oh, Mama." She held it against her shoulders.

"Try it on."

She ran into the bedroom where Lauren whirled around in her new dress. "Isn't it wonderful?"

"Yes. You look very pretty."

Lauren ran out of the room to show her parents.

Vivien shed her jeans and shirt. She went to the chest of

drawers and pulled out her crinoline. She stepped into it, then pulled the dress over her head. She strained to pull the zipper up the back but couldn't quite raise it all the way. Before she went into the living room to ask Mama to do it, she stood quite still, enjoying the feel of it. The soft, wool material had a sheen to it. She ran her hands down the sides, then went into the living room.

Mama's eyes lit up when she came in, and even Daddy smiled. Mama closed the zipper. "You look beautiful," she said. "Both of you." She turned to include Lauren. "My girls are growing up."

While they modeled, Mama told them they got the dresses for the school Christmas dance on Saturday. They could hardly wait.

At three in the afternoon, they all piled into the car again, and Daddy drove them to the officers' club. Cars arrived, dropped off kids, and drove away. There appeared to be more kids than they ever saw at school, everyone shouting and waving.

Inside, music played on the jukebox. A bartender handed out Cokes and other sodas. Bowls of chips and plates of cookies sat on each table beside small artificial Christmas trees. Mr. and Mrs. Gregerson and Miss Lawrence chaperoned. Every girl wore her fanciest dress or skirt, and the boys wore suits, making everyone almost unrecognizable. Vivien felt so grown up in her wool dress.

For a while, everyone milled around, eating and drinking. A few of the older kids danced to the music. Vivien sat at the table she'd staked out near the dance floor and watched.

Four o'clock came, and the adults handed out presents to all the kids. Amid shouts and laughter, the kids unwrapped packages, paper and bows flying everywhere. Everyone held their presents out to friends to show what they'd gotten. Vivien got a small German cuckoo clock. Lauren received a music box with a ballerina twirling on top. No two exactly alike in the whole room, Vivien saw. Looking around the room, she saw a dictionary, a small jewelry box, and more.

Her gaze lit on a girl sitting in a corner. Blonde hair, about Vivien's age, she didn't recognize her as a student on post. Her taffeta dress looked a little old-fashioned. It looked like she didn't receive a gift, yet she watched the others with a bright smile.

Vivien found Mr. Gregersen to tell him one girl didn't get a gift. "Where is she?" Mr. Gregersen asked. She pointed to the corner, only to see the chair sat empty.

"She must have gone to get a drink," she said.

"Send her to me when you find her."

She walked around looking for the girl. She wound around tables and chairs. Two couples danced awkwardly since most of them had never learned. She gave up on finding the girl and joined Lauren at the table. After a few moments, one of Lauren's friends came over and the two moved to sit with friends from her fourth-grade class.

Being alone at gatherings made Vivien uncomfortable. She didn't mix well with others, however, tonight, other students in the seventh and eighth grades gradually joined her. They joked and laughed and talked about whose music they liked best.

Richard Swiatek came up to Vivien. He'd graduated from the eighth-grade last year and moved away to the residential high school for ninth grade. "Let's dance," he said and held out his hand. His father, a major, served in Fontenet, and she'd met Richard at the Thanksgiving dinner. With his blond hair and nice clothes, she thought him one of the handsomest boys she'd ever seen.

She nearly choked on her Coke. "I don't really know how."

"I'll show you." She placed her hand in his and stood. His

fingers felt cool when he gently wrapped them around her hand.

"Just follow my lead," Richard said.

She tried but kept stumbling.

"Don't look down. Close your eyes and listen to the music."

She did. He stepped to the right—her right—and she followed. And the next step.

"My sister and I both took dance lessons," he said. "She's in college now and knowing how to dance is very important there."

He pulled her a little closer. She could feel his warmth. His hand on her waist. His breath on her cheek. He practically glided across the floor, and each moment she followed his lead more easily. The song ended.

"Thank you," he said when the music stopped.

"You're welcome."

The people she'd seen dancing in movies and on TV always looked so graceful. She let herself believe she and Richard had looked just as lovely.

He walked her back to the table, where he asked Samantha to dance to the next song. Resentment made Vivien clench her teeth. Stupid, she chided herself. After all, they hardly knew each other and certainly weren't dating.

She joined in the conversation about what clothes they all liked, and her mood lightened. Lauren danced with Robert Jackson. Or was he Anthony? The twins, sons of Daddy's first sergeant and children of a mixed marriage, were in the fifth grade, which put them in her building. No one paid any particular attention to them, one of whom now danced with Patty Spencer. So far, the brothers proved to be the best dancers in the room.

Couples moved about the dance floor all night. Vivien danced with Richard again and with one of the Jackson twins.

When not dancing, kids sat at a table or at the bar, drinking sodas and eating chips, feeling very grownup. Vivien checked the clock. Nearly 6:00.

A feeling of dread passed over her. The Gypsy woman mentioned danger in her future. She did not mention ghosts, but that must be what she referred to, given what happened back in the States. She'd yet to have an encounter in France and hoped there wouldn't be one. Her previous encounters with ghosts still brought bad dreams. She dreaded another experience.

At 6:00, she spotted the girl across the room. Her blonde hair almost glowed in the overhead light, making her stand out from all the others. She looked about twelve or thirteen, Vivien's age. The girl watched Richard and other high schoolers, who acted more sophisticated than the grade schoolers. They didn't mix with the younger students much, except for Richard, who moved from one group to another.

The stranger's gaze scanned the others with a studied air. She clearly did not fit in.

"Last dance," Mr. Gregerson called out.

Vivien nearly swooned when Richard asked her to dance to Pat Boone's soft, slow "Love Letters in the Sand."

CHRISTMAS MORNING, the girls woke early. They waited a while before waking their parents. The whole family loved Christmas, especially Daddy. He loved buying presents for Mama and the two of them, although Vivien had overheard Mama talking to him about spending so much money.

Daddy loved the lighter, and Mama said she'd use the stationery to write to her sister in the next few days. Lauren immediately wanted to write in her diary, but another present to unwrap lured her away.

At eleven, they piled into the car and headed to the mess hall for Christmas dinner. Instead of turkey, the cooks had prepared ham and appropriate side dishes. Everyone took seats along the long lines of tables and bowed their heads while the chaplain offered a prayer for the holiday season.

Again, they took home more than they'd eaten, including a large portion of an entire ham.

FIVE

Snow fell the first Monday after New Year's Day and the temperature dropped to near freezing. Everyone wore their coats in the classrooms until the furnace warmed up, usually after morning recess. The day of the snowfall, a snowball fight broke out during morning recess. Two of the teachers kept an eye on things to ensure no one got too aggressive.

By the end of the first week, everyone fell back into the routine. Vivien enjoyed Mr. Gregerson's way of teaching, and she studied hardest on Madame Guilbeau's French lessons. She wanted to learn to speak the language as well as she spoke English, although sometimes the difference in syntax nearly defeated her. For the first time, she learned "syntax" and "conjugate."

During the second week after the holiday, Vivien felt a little sick. They all thought it a simple cold, but it didn't go away. After a week of cold symptoms and fever, Mama took her to the dispensary on post. The Army doctor confirmed she had a cold. It hung on because the stress of moving and new surroundings had weakened her system. "She'll be right as rain in a week or two," he said. "Lots of chicken soup and rest will do the trick."

She continued going to school, and when she got home each day, she dropped onto the bed and fell asleep. When she threw up at school, Mama took her back to the clinic. The same doctor insisted it was only a cold.

The next morning, Vivien sat on the edge of the bed. The bedroom felt chilly as always, something she'd gotten used to. Lauren finished getting dressed and started toward the door. She stopped and turned to Vivien.

"You better hurry, Viv, or you'll be late."

"Okay."

Lauren left, and Vivien continued to sit there. She felt tired and weak, but she must get ready. She'd already missed too many days of school.

"Vivien?" Mama came in and sat beside her. "Still don't feel good?"

"No."

"I'm taking you to see the doctor again. This has gone on much too long."

Mama had tried everything, but nothing worked for very long. Her favorite remedy, Vicks Vaporub rubbed into her chest and neck with a sanitary napkin pinned around her neck overnight had helped the congestion, just not enough.

Mama called Daddy and he came home to pick them up. Lauren had caught the bus by the time he arrived, and they drove directly to the dispensary. He left the car for Mama to use, saying he would catch a ride home with a friend that afternoon. Although the dispensary stayed open twenty-four hours, they didn't take regular appointments until eight o'clock. Vivien was first in line.

Another doctor saw her. After Mama explained that Vivien had been sick for more than two weeks, and after the usual examination, he ordered a chest x-ray. Vivien curled up on the examination table and nearly went to sleep before the doctor returned. Mama helped her sit up.

"Looks like she has walking pneumonia," he said. "The fact it's lingering is what makes her feel so bad. We'll give her a shot of penicillin. You can take her home but keep an eye on her. She'll need another shot if she hasn't improved by the end of the week."

As much as Vivien hated getting shots, if this one helped, she would be ecstatic. He also prescribed aspirin for the fever and plenty of liquids and soup. "Lots of rest," he said and sent them on their way.

Back home, Vivien drank some orange juice. She undressed and crawled into bed, waking only when Daddy came home. "What did the doctor say?" she heard him ask. She couldn't hear Mama's muffled response. Lauren had come home earlier and changed clothes. Vivien only vaguely remembered her being in the room.

Mama got her up and helped her put on her robe. While the rest ate meat loaf and mashed potatoes, she drank hot chicken soup. Between the soup and her fever, she felt like she was burning up.

"Can I have some ice cream?" She imagined it, cold and creamy in her dry mouth and sore throat.

"No," Mama said. "Any milk-type foods will only make your congestion worse. You can have juice. We have orange or prune juice. Water and ice will help your throat."

She wanted to take off the robe and pour cold water over her body. Instead, she drank another small glass of orange juice.

"Back to bed?" Mama asked.

"Yes, please."

The sheets had cooled, and they felt wonderful against her

hot skin. Mama brought a glass of ice water and set it on the bedside table. She sat next to her daughter and placed a cold wet washcloth on her forehead. Vivien fell into a fitful sleep.

At first, she tossed and turned, unable to get comfortable. She woke herself, talking to someone, or no one. Lauren came in once and asked how she felt. Whether she answered or not she couldn't remember. Finally, she fell into a deep sleep.

She woke again in the early morning and turned her head to check the time. She couldn't see the glow of the clock dial. She felt so much better and climbed out of bed. When she reached for the bedside lamp, her fingers couldn't find it. Strange. Mama must have moved it to make room for the water glass. Carefully, she passed her hand over the table, feeling for the glass. And found nothing at all.

Why did Mama take everything away? Maybe she'd been thrashing around so much, Mama feared things might get broken. Vivien sat down on the side of the bed, confused. She needed to turn on the ceiling light but didn't want to waken Lauren. She'd figure it out in the morning.

She lay back down and covered up. Wanting to look out the tall windows, she doubled the feather pillow to raise her head. Stars twinkled in the black sky. It wouldn't be long before the sun rose, shining through their window to waken them.

A flash of white flew at the window. It veered off at the last minute and disappeared to the right. It had to be a large bird, perhaps an owl. Its appearance both scared and amazed her. Hadn't she read somewhere that seeing an owl meant someone would die? No, not in this house. Not now. Please.

She woke again with the feeling only minutes had passed. Someone sat on the edge of the bed beside her.

"Mama."

"I'm so sorry you're sick," a strange voice said. "I was that sick once." It was a child's voice.

Vivien pushed with her feet against the mattress until her head pressed against the headboard of the bed. She pulled the bed covers up to her chin.

"Who are you? What are you doing on my bed?"

"I didn't mean to frighten you. In fact, I didn't think you'd wake up."

"Who are you?"

"My name is Mignon Cuvier."

"Why are you here?"

"I wanted to see if you are all right."

"I'm fine. And if you don't leave, I'll call my father."

"I thought you would have already."

"He'll beat you silly."

"No, he won't. He won't even see me."

Vivien bit her lip and gripped the blankets tighter. Was the girl saying she was a ghost? A living girl or a ghost? Which could be worse?

"Did I see you at the Christmas party?"

"I knew you saw me. I kept moving out of your line of sight. Finally, I had to leave, although I enjoyed the party so much."

"I don't want you here." Vivien shifted under the covers.

"I know. But I'm so lonely. Do you know you're the only person to see me in years?"

"Why are you still here?"

"Among the living, you mean? I'm not sure. I died when I was thirteen."

There hadn't been a peep out of Lauren during this whole conversation. Vivien reached over to the other side of the bed. Her sister wasn't there. Mama probably had her sleeping on the sofa in the living room so they both could get some sleep.

"Please go away," Vivien said. "I don't want to deal with a ghost. We haven't been here long and everything's strange enough." The girl didn't say anything, and Vivien waited a few moments. "Please, Mignon."

The cuckoo clock in the living room ticked off the silence. Finally, the voice said, "All right. For now. I will be back, though."

"No—"

Her weight lifted from the side of the bed. Vivien waved her arms around in the dark and touched nothing and no one. She looked toward the bedside table. The numbers on the dial of the clock glowed. The lamp sat where it should.

She scooted back under the covers. Had the girl been real? Maybe her fever had her imagining someone there. It would be wonderful if true.

IN SPITE of the cold temperature, kids ran around, hollering to each other. Some played with a ball, some sort of soccer game. Two girls played the latest clapping game, which always appeared out of nowhere, had no names, and disappeared as soon as a new one came along.

Vivien sat on the bench next to the main building and watched. Although the pneumonia had finally gone away, she needed to regain her strength before she could run around like the others.

She'd been back to school two days now and glad of it. A rare kid who loved school, she also hated being unable to play. The doctor said it wouldn't be long. Meanwhile, she concentrated on the French lessons. Madame Guilbeau helped her sometimes when they both had free time. The French teacher never joked or made comments, but she appreciated Vivien's desire to learn her language. She lent her books to help with dialogue and syntax and wrote out extra lessons.

Madame complimented her accent and encouraged Vivien to speak French whenever she went shopping with the family or on school trips. So far, she hadn't worked up the courage to say more than "*Merci*," and "*Bonjour*." It must be silly to worry so much about making a mistake, but it kept people from laughing at her feeble attempts.

Vivien looked up from the book to watch kids kick a ball around. The ball got away and rolled toward the fence. In a second, it rolled back the way it came. Mignon had kicked it. The kids probably believed it hit the fence and bounced back. The young ghost looked over and smiled, which faded quickly.

The blonde hair and ice blue eyes, fair complexion, even the slightly old-fashioned clothes added to the look of a young girl of another time. Were her parents still alive? Did someone else look out for her? When they had talked the other night, Vivien felt that Mignon tried to sound older, confident, to give the impression she was more mature. What dangers or discomforts would a young ghost face?

Vivien looked around at the kids in the yard, all safe and

alive. They had families and rarely found themselves alone or lonely.

The bell rang and Vivien stood and looked toward the fence. No one stood next to it. She walked inside, wondering how a young French girl could speak English so well. If only she wasn't a ghost.

The bus stopped in the parking lot of St. Eutrope Basilica in Saintes. It was mid-morning, and they were on the first school trip for upper grades of the Fontenet school in the new year. Mr. Gregerson recited facts about the church during the drive from the school.

"Originally, Benedictines built a monastery and a two-story church in the ninth century. In the eleventh century, they enlarged it, and it became a basilica honoring St. Eutrope, the first bishop of Saintes."

That meant a large stone building, dark inside, maybe with stained-glass windows, according to Samantha. Now in her second year in France, and in the eighth grade, her family would rotate back to the States in the summer. She seemed very happy about getting back to "the land of the round door-knob," as Americans called their home country. Most doors in this part of France used oval doorknobs.

Everyone tumbled out of the bus laughing and talking. Once everyone had gathered, Mr. Gregerson counted them once more. Twelve altogether. "Follow me," he said and led them along a brick sidewalk to the red, wooden door of the entrance. Narrow, probably not wide enough for a wheelchair, it seemed very ordinary for such an important building.

Within seconds, everyone spoke in whispers and tiptoed to keep the sounds of their presence from bouncing off the stone walls. Their lowered voices surrounded the group in ghost whispers. Mr. Gregerson led the way along the back of the large open space of the main sanctuary. He stopped at the center aisle. Wooden benches lined up in rows from the back and wooden chairs nearest the altar.

"We are in the nave of the basilica," he said. Mr. Gregerson stood a moment, letting his charges gather closer around him.

"Now," he said, "this is a basilica, not a cathedral." He went on to explain the differences between the two. "The general term for places of worship, no matter how grand, is church. The word also designates groups of believers or followers."

Vivien stepped away from the crowd and turned her attention to the windows above the main altar. Not much else could be seen in the way of decoration except what lay on and around the altar and the small stained-glass windows. They added color but little brightness, twilight being the rule inside. She scanned the ceiling and walls for electric lights. There were none. Services on cloudy days must be very dark.

Mr. Gregerson led them down the center aisle toward the altar. "Notice the smaller altars on either side," he said. "In 1562, France's religious wars began between Catholics and Protestants." They reached the area in front of the altar, and he stopped walking, continuing to describe Protestants seeking refuge within the basilica.

Vivien wandered to the left side, still hearing every word. A stone arch opened into the smaller altar which stood against one wall with several chairs facing it. Large candlesticks, an altar cloth, and other paraphernalia lay on the altar, including a small statue of Mary in the center. Surely the priest didn't give sermons from here.

When she turned to leave, she saw someone sitting in one of the chairs with her head down appearing to pray. She started to apologize for disturbing her, and stopped when the small figure raised her head to reveal Mignon.

"What do you think?" she asked.

"Shhh, they'll hear you."

"Who?" The ghost smiled. "No one can hear me except you. Listen. Does my voice echo like everyone else's?"

She listened. Mr. Gregerson's voice still came clearly. The whisper of footsteps brushed the walls. Thankfully, Mignon's voice had not carried.

"See. I can talk, but you must be careful. They'll think you're crazy if you talk to me."

"Thanks a lot."

She smiled. "How are you enjoying this visit to the past?"

"I love . . . You're trying to embarrass me."

Vivien looked to the gathering being led back the way they came. No one looked her way.

"I have to go."

"We could go outside and talk."

"I don't want to talk. I want to hear about this church."

"Basilica."

Vivien hurried out and joined the group for the rest of the tour. No one associated with the basilica itself joined them to tell of its history. Mr. Gregerson seemed to know it well. He led them down some steps into the crypt with even dimmer light and a low-ceilinged forest of columns. In the center stood a small stone tomb where St. Eutrope's remains lay.

"The crypt is closed now, so no new burials," Mr. Gregerson said.

Vivien found herself distracted, watching for Mignon to

reappear. She needed to be alert for her next appearance so she wouldn't embarrass herself by reacting. If only she knew of some way to be rid of her or at least limit her appearing whenever and wherever she wanted.

When they boarded the bus for the return trip to school, Mignon sat in the back. Vivien tried to ignore her presence. After a while, though, she couldn't resist turning around. She'd disappeared.

After dinner that evening, Vivien sat on the low stone wall around the old well in the back yard. She kept hoping the Gypsies, who had left right after the first of the year, would return. She wanted to ask the old woman what she knew about Mignon.

She felt Mignon's presence before seeing her, barely visible in the twilight. The ghost walked through the shaft of light from the kitchen window to sit on the wall next to her. Vivien wanted to reach out to see if she was as solid as she looked.

"I didn't mean to embarrass you today."

"Good." She sounded angry. She felt angry. Should she be sorry?

"It really will be best if you only appear when I'm alone. Like I told you the other night, my family and I have enough to worry about and get used to."

"I'm not your first."

"First? You mean ghost?" She could barely see Mignon smile. "Who are you? Not just your name. Are you French? American? I know your name is French."

Mignon shrugged. "It no longer matters."

"It does to me."

"Why?"

Why did it matter? She understood what she said, but did that mean she always spoke English? She couldn't hear an accent. "Do you speak French?"

"If you like."

"Never mind." Vivien got to her feet. "I have homework to do."

"*Bon soir.*"

"Good night."

Mignon didn't appear the rest of the night. Vivien finished her homework in spite of the distraction of worrying about the ghost appearing again. Later, lying in bed, she found herself wishing the girl was real. In spite of the short amount of time since Mignon first appeared, Vivien found the girl fascinating and wanted to see more of her. But her feelings were mixed, since she didn't consider another encounter with a ghost something to look forward to.

In the earlier encounters with ghosts, she'd told her mother very little, knowing she could not share the experience. For some reason, she desperately wanted to tell Mama everything she knew about Mignon. Yet, she had so little she could say.

EIGHT

January cold seemed to go on forever. At school, Mr. Gregerson pronounced some days too cold for the kids to play outside. The school buildings did not have one room large enough for everyone, so they sat at their desks and played games the teachers provided. Checkers and other board games, such as The Last Straw, were popular, and Pick-Up-Stix, and card games. The younger kids liked Go Fish. Vivien enjoyed Chinese Checkers.

They sometimes went to the gym on post and jumped on the trampoline while the older boys shot baskets on half-court. Since they had to walk from the school, they only went on warmer days.

The school buildings might be less than ideal, although Mama expressed surprise at the new textbooks when they first started school. She'd expected a bit less—older books, or perhaps fewer—since the school system had existed for less than five years. As for Vivien, being in a classroom with an older class didn't bother her at all. She loved to listen when Mr.

Gregersen taught the eighth graders. Except when it came to math, where she felt hopeless. She found English and history a breeze, as usual. She didn't always absorb geography, although it included information on other societies. She enjoyed that part.

Among the books she checked out of the libraries, she always picked up one or two on the history of France. Nothing like a textbook, mostly biographies of kings and queens, one or two about Napoleon, and one on French colonial history. She'd heard her parents discussing "the situation in Algeria," which was difficult to understand—some sort of fighting, the Algerians wanting independence from the French. The books said the Algerians were so much better off as part of a larger, more advanced nation, so why did they want the French to leave?

Every so often, they all got in the car and drove up to St. Jean on a Saturday to shop in Les Galleries, the large department store. It had become habit for Vivien to go off with Mama and Lauren to shop with Daddy. Mama spoke no French at all, yet she'd made friends with one of the saleswomen who spoke a little English. Between that and Mama's hand signs, they got along famously.

One Saturday they went to Les Galleries to look for a side table Mama wanted for the living room. Daddy went off to look for a new belt with Lauren by his side. Vivien saw a jewelry counter and wandered away from Mama while keeping her in sight. She'd taken to wearing the pendant the Gypsy woman gave her and wondered if there might be a ring or bracelet to match.

The saleswoman behind the counter approached. *"C'est jolie."* That's pretty, she said, pointing at the pendant.

"Merci." Vivien touched the pendant.

"Americaine?"

"*Oui.*"

The woman smiled and Vivien returned it, relieved to find the woman friendly. She'd run into a few unfriendly French people, not fond of Americans living among them. She didn't hang around when she did.

"*Parlez-vous anglais?*"

"*Oui, un petit peu.*" A little bit.

Vivien felt so proud to understand even that little bit of the language.

"May I show you something?" The woman waved a hand indicating the glass cases.

"Oh, no. I just wanted to look." She looked down at the display in the glass case. "So many pretty things." She looked up at the woman and took a step backward. Behind the woman stood shadowy figures of children, wavering as if a breeze blew across a column of smoke.

The woman looked behind herself. "They will not hurt you. We recognize your, how you say, talent?"

"You are—"

"Yes, I am. Be well, be careful, Vivien."

"Vivien? There you are."

Her mother's voice brought her around to face her. "Mama."

"What's wrong?"

Vivien looked back toward the jewelry counter. She saw nothing behind it. She described what she'd seen.

"Is that the first time you've seen a group like that?"

"Yes. Why would . . . I've no idea . . ."

"I don't know, darling. It sounds like they meant no harm."

"They didn't. I wasn't afraid."

Daddy and Lauren approached. He held up a black leather belt, and Lauren had a small doll. Mama led them to the side table she'd found.

"Didn't you find anything, Viv?" Daddy asked.

"She found a ring she liked," Mama said. "I told her we might get it for her birthday."

Daddy smiled. "We'll see."

They paid for their purchases. While she waited, Vivien looked back the way they had come. The woman from the jewelry counter reappeared, waved once, and with a smile faded away.

When they got home, Vivien went straight to the bedroom to write down what happened in her new diary. She'd liked the one she gave Lauren for Christmas so much, she bought one for herself the last time they went shopping. The days and months were in French, and she tried to write at least one sentence each day in French.

She wrote the first sentence in French.

Nous sommes allés à St. Jean aujourd'hui.

We went to St. Jean today.

Continuing in English, she described what she saw. At the end of the entry, she added:

The woman said, "Be well, be careful, Vivien."
Why would she say that? Was there danger?

The sight of the gathering of ghosts had startled her. She'd never seen so many at one time before, but she didn't feel the woman and the others meant her any harm.

She closed her eyes and pictured her. A pretty woman, her brown hair styled a little old-fashioned, like her suit and blouse. A pleasant voice and she spoke English with a French accent. Red lipstick. And flowery scent. How could she detect scent?

Curiously, Mignon hadn't appeared for a few days. And today the woman and her host of children appeared.

CHAPTER

NINE

On Sunday, the newspapers had been read and the crossword cut out, to be tried later. Vivien asked if she could go for a walk around the village.

"It's very cold out there," Mama said.

"I know. But the sun is shining, and my coat is warm enough."

"And your new boots," Daddy said. He'd teased her about wanting to wear them all the time since she opened the package on Christmas. They looked so sophisticated with wedge heels, black suede, and fancy shoestrings.

"All right," Mama said, "be careful. And don't tire yourself out. You're still recovering from pneumonia."

Vivien raced to get ready before they changed their minds. First, the boots, then the long coat from Sears and Roebuck store in Nashville. Last, a scarf tied around her head. Mama always reminded her that people lost most body heat through the tops of their heads. While she got ready, Lauren told her she was crazy to go out in the cold.

"The sun's shining," Vivien said.

"That doesn't make it any warmer."

"I'm okay," Vivien said and headed for the door. She stood on the stoop a moment, enjoying the bright sun. She pulled her gloves from the large pockets and bounced down the steps. The large metal gate squealed like always even though she only opened it a few inches. She squeezed through and stood, deciding whether to turn right toward the cemetery or left toward the church.

She'd always enjoyed walking through cemeteries, reading tombstones. Those of children always made her sad, and there were also stones of people who lived long lives. Sometimes funny sayings had been carved into the stones.

However much the cemetery attracted her, she turned left instead toward the church. She saw no one else as she alternately walked and skipped. Her nose got cold quickly, though the rest of her stayed warm enough. Out of sight of the house, she pulled the scarf off and wadded it up into the coat pocket. She hated wearing it. Someday, she'd like to buy a fur hat for cold weather.

The church sat quiet when she reached it. Most people in the village went to church every Sunday. Many of them walked past her house, men and women chattering, and children skipping ahead and back. Afterward, they must go home and eat big meals and fall asleep in their easy chairs for the village looked abandoned on Sunday afternoons. No one walked or cycled on the sidewalks or streets. Now, mid-afternoon, not a person or vehicle was in sight.

She looked at windows as she passed a few businesses and a few homes, the curtains drawn, no one peeking out. She passed the bakery, where she sometimes went for bread, and the café on the corner across from the churchyard. Since she'd never been inside the café, she thought about going in now. She decided against it since they probably only served wine and she didn't have any money with her. Not that she wanted wine, of course.

She crossed the street and passed by the large grassy area on the north side of the church. A few trees grew there, and a concrete bench sat under them, not too welcoming in the cold. Past the church to the south side ran a narrow alley. In front of the church entrance, a wide concrete sidewalk spread from the curb to a narrower sidewalk curving toward the light blue doors. The doors stood open.

She looked around to see if anyone might be watching. Seeing no one, she went to the door and leaned in. It took a long moment for her eyes to adjust to the dark interior. No one inside as far as she could see. She stepped inside.

The stone walls looked cold, but the air felt warm on her face. The sound of her footsteps echoed and filled the space. When she stopped moving, complete silence surrounded her. It smelled of dust and candlewax. Studying the interior, she could see no heat source, yet something had warmed the space, perhaps the warmth of dozens of people from morning services, plus the candles burning near the altar.

The stone floor stretched from doorway to the altar. Wooden pews lined each side of the wide center aisle with traces of color from having been painted many years ago. A few chairs sat scattered about near the altar. Three stained-glass windows in the far wall over the altar let in light, the center window twice as wide as the ones to either side, each no more than ten inches wide. Framed religious scenes hung on the side walls. Two religious figures sat on pedestals on either side of the altar in the center of a raised dais. A cloth lay across the altar with more religious articles and candlesticks placed on top of it.

Vivien had never been inside a Catholic church before coming to France. Although smaller than the basilica in

Saintes, certain things were the same: lots of religious items on the altar, candles burning, the smell of an old building. Baptist churches she'd been to had none of those, only the occasional pictures of a blond Jesus.

A feeling of peace and many centuries settled over her. She had no idea how old the church might be, but it felt very old. There'd been no plaque on the outside wall giving the name and date of building, so she looked for one inside on the walls beside the doors.

"The church is called Église Saint-Médard," a voice said. Vivien looked back toward the altar. Mignon stood beside one of the pews on the right. "Originally built in the twelfth century, practically destroyed in the fourteenth, and rebuilt in the nineteenth century." She came nearer. "Looks older, doesn't it?"

"Yes, it looks and feels like it's been here for a thousand years."

Mignon held out her hand. "Come in and look more closely. There's nothing of any particular value. It is a poor provincial church, after all. Nothing very lovely either."

The words made Vivien angry. What right did the girl have to criticize the church like that?

Nevertheless, Vivien followed the ghost toward the altar. She stopped when she spied a smaller space to the right, a niche large enough for a small altar and a couple of chairs. A larger window crisscrossed with blue lines was placed high in the wall. On a pedestal atop a shelf behind the altar sat a pure white Madonna figure holding baby Jesus.

"That's beautiful," Vivien said. She glanced at Mignon to see her expression.

"True."

Although other pieces sat on the altar and shelf—a small, more colorful figure, and a silver candlestick among them—

she only had eyes for the Madonna. The beauty of it. Never very religious, she still would have liked to take the piece home.

"You want it?"

Mignon's voice brought her back to where they stood.

"It's beautiful."

The girl took her hand and led her toward the main altar. "There's more to see." Mignon told her about the religious wars in France from 1562 to 1598 between Catholics and Huguenots. Many Huguenots occupied western France. Long before that, however, this church and others like it became sanctuaries for pilgrims traveling from northern France and England to holy places to the south, Spain, Italy, and Portugal.

Vivien hung on every word, mentally picturing rich and poor, peasant and noble traveling together. The priests opening the doors of the church. Voices speaking in hushed tones. She'd studied French history back in Manchester during the year they lived with Grandma and read more books since moving here. These details made it live.

A sudden look of anger came over Mignon's face.

"*Bonjour. Puis-je vous aider?*"

Vivien whirled around at the sound of an unfamiliar voice.

"*Excusez moi,*" she said.

A priest in a black cassock stood just inside the door, looking at her curiously. "*Êtes-vous américaine?* You are American?"

He was slender, of average height, and could have been young or middle-aged. His hair was brown with a receding hairline on either side of a pronounced widow's peak.

"*Oui.* You speak English?"

"*Oui.* Not well."

"I'm sorry if I intruded. I have never been here and just

wanted . . ." She'd been curious. Was it an acceptable reason for invading a church? "We live up the street. In the purple house."

"Ah, *bon*. We welcome all. May I help with any information?"

"*Merci, non.* I need to get back home."

The priest looked around the sanctuary. "You are alone?"

"*Oui.*"

"I thought . . . *ça ne fait rien.* Just thought I heard someone else."

"No, just me."

He came closer and held out his hand. "*Je suis* Pere Antoine."

"*Je m'appelle* Vivien," she said, remembering the formal words. They shook hands and she walked to the door. When she reached it, he called out, "Come back when you wish."

She thanked him again and stepped outside. When Father Antoine spoke the first time, she felt as if his voice snapped her out of a dream. She'd been so engrossed in Mignon's history lesson. Had she been hypnotized? Had the father seen Mignon? Or heard her?

The sun sat lower in the sky and the air had gotten colder. She tied the scarf around her head again to protect her ears from the wind and please her mother that she'd worn it. Later that night, she wondered again if Father Antoine had seen or heard Mignon. A more worrying thought came to her. Would the good father think her possessed or wicked if he did?

In the quiet hours of early morning, Vivien lay in bed, unable to sleep. She kept thinking about how Mignon acted and many other things, all becoming mixed up in her head. She reminded herself the girl was a ghost, whether good or bad, she couldn't say. The lady ghost in the department store told her to be careful. Had she referred to Mignon? Or the Gypsy, perhaps?

Most of the time, Mignon acted friendly, or teasing. At least it seemed to be teasing. Sometimes she acted superior, making her seem a little older.

Month after next, in March, Vivien would turn thirteen. She liked boys and often thought about dancing with Richard Swiatek. He'd seemed more mature than the boys in her class and acted as if he liked her. She'd made very few friends at school, although they all played together at recess, which made her wonder why Mignon came to her. The other ghosts —the nurse in Breckinridge, the Japanese girl in Manchester— wanted help in solving their problems. So far, this new ghost acted like she wanted to be her friend.

So many thoughts keeping her awake. She came back to, what did Mignon want?

The girl hadn't asked for anything or said anything about a problem in her life or death to be solved. Vivien had begun to like her very much. If only she didn't get snippy sometimes.

Vivien rolled over onto her side in frustration. Until Mignon told her the problem—if she had a problem—and asked for help, she'd have to wait. That's the way it was in the first two encounters.

Something rattled against the glass of the window. She sat up, listening. It came again. Throwing the covers back, she stepped into her slippers and padded to the window to look out. The nearly full moon lit up the back yard. Standing beneath the window, Mignon motioned for her to come out.

She shook her head. It was late and cold, and Daddy would most likely hear the door open and close. He would be angry. Maybe she could pretend she'd walked in her sleep, although she never had before. Mignon stretched out her hands, pleading.

Why not go? The door didn't squeak when opened slowly. They'd been in bed a couple of hours, so Daddy must be sound asleep. She looked back at the bed. Lauren was just a lump under the covers. They always kept the bedroom doors closed to hold in the heat from the fireplaces in the corner, now with only glowing hot coals.

She held up one finger, telling Mignon to wait. She grabbed her chenille bathrobe and put it on as she went to the door. It opened silently. She stepped into the hall and closed the door behind her. Slowly and softly, she walked to the front door. The doorknob in the center of the door operated the exposed mechanism and made only a slight noise .

She slipped outside and closed the door softly behind her.

Mignon appeared at the base of the steps leading down toward the back yard. Vivien rushed down, shivering. Mignon embraced her.

"I'm so glad you came out," she murmured.

"Really?"

Mignon chuckled. "Really."

"Why?" She stepped back to look into Mignon's eyes, but the ghost led her to the old well and gently pulled her down to sit on the edge. The cold of the stones penetrated the robe and nightgown, and she shivered.

"It's too cold," Vivien said.

"You will warm up in a moment." Mignon, in a soft dress and a thin wool coat, didn't seem to feel the cold at all. "I'm so glad you came. I have something for you."

"What?"

The ghost held out her right hand balled into a fist. She raised Vivien's hand under her own and something cold dropped into it. Vivien held her hand so the moonlight shone on what looked like a metal pendant on a chain. With her other hand, numb with cold, she picked it up carefully between two fingers. The pendant was round and enameled, blue in the center, circled by white, with an outer circle of red. The whole disk was pleated like a fan, giving it an uneven surface. She guessed it measured about an inch across. The chain appeared to be gold, although probably a cheaper metal.

"It's beautiful."

"It's a French cockade. Everyone wore them during and after the revolution. Made of cloth, of course. Let me help you take your old one off so you can put it on."

"No." Vivien hadn't meant to speak so sharply. "I never take this off." She took the talisman in her right hand.

"I know, but you can't wear both."

"Just help me put it on." She held the two ends of the chain behind her neck and faced away.

"Better not to wear it at all."

"Don't be angry. It's just that I promised."

"A promise made to someone more important than me." She sounded sulky.

Vivien wanted to soothe her wounded feelings but had no intention of taking off the talisman. "No, please. Fasten it for me."

Mignon did so. The pendant settled just below the neck of her nightgown. It felt cold through the flannel. She took it between her fingers again, her hand almost too cold to feel the pleats.

"Thank you. It's wonderful." Mignon didn't respond. "I think I'd better get back inside. It's just so cold."

"Do what you will."

"Will you come back tomorrow?"

"Maybe. I don't know."

Vivien stood and took two steps toward the stairs. Mignon put her hand on her shoulder. Vivien turned, and Mignon kissed her on both cheeks with feather light lips. Vivien felt forgiven.

"Go on."

Mignon's expression softened, and Vivien nodded. She hurried back into the house. Before getting into bed, she went to the window. Mignon stood below looking toward the moon. Slowly, her shape faded and disappeared.

Vivien shivered. She slipped under the covers of the bed, resisting the temptation to spoon with Lauren to get warm. As cold as she was, Lauren would waken at the slightest touch and ask questions. Gradually, her body warmed under the wool army blankets. However, the metal pendant remained uncomfortably cold to the touch. She undid the catch and laid it on her bedside table.

Her clock cuckooed twice in the living room before she drifted to sleep. She dreamed of Mignon and the French revolution. She stood in the center of a mob shouting for . . . what? Her knowledge of French didn't include the words they used, as the people shook their fists and shouted in anger.

CHAPTER

ELEVEN

Vivien drew the covers over her head. Mama had turned on the overhead light to waken her and Lauren. It had always been her method of getting them out of bed. This morning, it made Vivien angry.

She'd been up late last night with Mignon again. The third night in a row. Vivien needed more sleep, and lack of it made her irritable. If the ghost appeared tonight, she must ask her not to come again for a while. She couldn't let this interfere with her getting good grades.

Vivien had always been competitive when it came to school. She might not have the highest grade on every assignment or at the end of each semester, but she always tried her best. More than anything, she wanted to go to college, and good grades would be essential. Not that she had much of a chance. Her parents certainly could not afford the tuition, but she would at least do her part in case things changed.

Remembering today was Friday cheered her up. Mama let her sleep late on Saturdays, at least until nine o'clock. Sometimes she wakened to the sound of the washing machine in the basement directly below the bedroom. She hated the whoosh-whoosh sound.

Tomorrow, Daddy had to be on duty so it would be the three of them busy cleaning and hanging up the wash.

Vivien fell asleep on the bus in spite of its being so cold inside. She woke still in darkness when the bus stopped to pick up two kids, a brother and sister. The girl was in Lauren's fourth grade class, and the two chatted cheerfully. The boy, in second grade, was left to his own devices the same as Vivien. The bus had warmed up, and Vivien sat up straight to chase away sleep. In another few minutes, the sky lightened in the east. She might not like getting up early in the morning, but seeing the sky in the east gradually brighten with sunrise on a clear crisp day lightened her mood.

The janitor turned up the furnace an hour before classes started, and the buildings warmed reluctantly, leaving the classroom cold for the next hour. All the students wore their coats, and some kept their gloves on. Morning recess came and everyone trooped outside, glad to be moving, stamping cold feet to renew circulation in numb toes.

Once, through the crowd of kids, Vivien thought she saw Mignon on the other side of the playground. When she worked her way over, she saw no sign of her. She felt for the French cockade pendant, remembered it lay on her bedside table. What if Mama sees it when she cleans? Maybe she wouldn't clean their bedroom today. Mama hadn't mentioned it so far. She and Lauren always made their own bed and straightened up before they left each morning, so there wasn't much else to do. Please, don't let her see it.

When they went back inside, the furnace had warmed the classroom, and everyone took off coats and gloves. Vivien looked forward to afternoon recess and working on French with Madame Guilbeau, who insisted they continue working on conjugating verbs. When the French teacher first used the word "conjugate," the students had been confused. Although she'd never had any English teacher use the word or recite "I am, you are . . ." Vivien figured out what it meant while they repeated the words.

She sat outside on the bench next to the building. The sun shone brightly, and it felt good to be outside. Today Madame chose the verb *avoir*, to have. *J'ai. Vous as. Il a. Nous avons. Vous avez. Ils avaient.* So far, they only went over present tense. Vivien suspected past tense and future tense would be harder.

While she repeated the words aloud, she scanned the playground. No sign of Mignon.

On the bus that afternoon, Vivien thought about her feelings toward the ghost. They hadn't known each other very long. She missed the girl when she didn't see her. When she appeared, the girl made her feel . . . afraid? Uneasy? As though she waited for something to happen. She liked Mignon and had come to think of her as her best friend. She was afraid of saying or doing something that would make Mignon not like her anymore.

She never had many friends. Oh, she played with girls near her age—the hand clapping games and kicking a ball around. Lauren made friends so easily, friends who came to the house to play or she would visit them. All the while, Vivien read, did homework, and visited the church on Sunday.

When she got home, Vivien went into the bedroom and put on the pendant. In the kitchen, she helped fix supper by cutting up lettuce and tomato for salad.

"Where did that come from?" Mama asked.

"What?"

"The necklace. Is it to do with the American flag?"

Vivien held it up. "No, ma'am. It's a French cockade."

"Did someone give it to you?"

"I found it." Vivien crossed her fingers behind her back.

"Where?"

"When I went for my walk Sunday. I saw it lying on the sidewalk."

"May I see it?"

Vivien unfastened it and lay it in Mama's hand.

"I think it's gold." Mama turned it over and looked at the back, holding it so the light shone on it. "It's not a cheap necklace."

"Oh."

"Maybe we should try to find out who it belongs to."

"It probably belongs to someone here in the village. How would we find out who?"

"Let me think about it."

Vivien took it into her room and put it into the velvet box she used to hold a couple of rings and a bracelet. She didn't have enough jewelry to need a real jewelry box. Maybe if Mama didn't see it again, she'd forget about finding out who lost it.

She took her book into the living room and draped herself over the arm of the overstuffed chair. Having become curious about the French revolution, she looked for and found a book in the school library. She skipped the earlier history and went directly to the revolution in the eighteenth century. The French rebelled against the monarchy, mimicking the American revolution, but things got terribly out of hand.

The text gave few specifics. Still, the brutality came through. Madame Guillotine, heads rolling, spies everywhere. What a terrible time to live.

Mama called out for her and Lauren to set the table for supper. Daddy got home before they finished. After they ate and cleaned up the kitchen, Vivien returned to the book. A disturbing question grew in her mind, and when she'd finished reading, she considered it. Did Mignon die in the revolution?

Her mode of dress seemed older, but not that old, and she spoke like most of the other kids, although sometimes with an odd turn of phrase. English wasn't her first language. Madame Guilbeau, for all her education and skill with English, spoke oddly at times, too.

Being Friday night, Lauren and Vivien stayed up until ten o'clock rather than nine. Daddy suggested a game of hearts, the card game he almost always won. Everyone agreed, partly to have something to do, and they all loved playing card games. One day they hoped to finally beat him. He always laughed at the idea.

In the last game, Lauren got stuck with the queen of spades. "Not fair!"

"You know you can't beat the old man," Daddy said and laughed.

He went on to list the mistakes she'd made. He explained how cards should be played if someone wanted to leave everyone with all the points. Vivien always marveled at how he could remember every card played. He could do the same when he and Mama played pinochle with another couple one Saturday a month.

Mama especially enjoyed those evenings since she rarely got out to socialize. Daddy almost always needed the car, and most other American families lived in military housing, where they had American neighbors. Mama must feel lonely at times. That thought turned into wondering the same about Mignon. Did she seek company because of loneliness?

She looked out the window, surprised to see the moon rising. She nearly cried out when she realized it wasn't the moon. Mignon's face, close to the window, rose slowly until she looked Vivien straight in the eye. She had the saddest expression.

Vivien couldn't turn away from the apparition. Horror gripped her. Mignon's face, glowing against the dark sky with no body below it.

How could there be a head and no body? Even for a ghost that was weird.

Madame Guillotine came to mind. The blade coming down, people's heads dropping into baskets below. Crowds cheering.

Mignon gave the smallest of smiles and disappeared.

"Vivien, what's the matter?"

Mama's voice penetrated Vivien's panic, and she looked around at her family.

"N-nothing. I was listening to Daddy."

Her parents looked at each other and back at her. Vivien saw that Lauren had left the table and the cards had been put away. None of them could have seen anything except her own startled reaction.

"Off to bed with you," Mama said. She looked concerned, and Vivien expected she'd get a visit once she climbed into bed.

Daddy came rather than Mama. He sat on the side of the bed and put his hand on her forehead. "Was tonight one of those times when you are deep in thought?" He brushed her hair back from her face.

"Yes. Nothing really."

"Your mama worries."

"I know."

"I worry, too."

"I know." She didn't really know that. Daddy often seemed too distant, preoccupied with being a soldier.

"You're all right?"

"Yes."

"Good." He leaned down and kissed her cheek. "Good night."

"'Night."

He left the room and closed the door. The moment of silence was short.

"Viv?" Lauren lay facing away.

Vivien grunted. She'd thought Lauren was asleep.

"Are you okay?"

"Yes, I'm okay. Are you worried about me, too?"

"No. Well, maybe a little."

Vivien turned onto her right side and patted Lauren on the back. "Go to sleep." She pulled the covers over her head for the warmth and to block out any sound, like the tick-tick of small gravel hitting the windows thrown by Mignon. She wanted to think about Daddy. She never doubted he loved her and Lauren, although he rarely showed it. Without much effort, he made her feel safe. When he wasn't around, she knew he soon would be. Tonight, he'd surprised her.

Next morning, during recess, Mignon appeared in the play-ground. She acted as if she were playing with some of the other kids. They didn't see her, of course. When the ghost looked her way, Vivien turned her head. She joined other girls who practiced a new hand clapping game, one she hadn't tried yet. They showed her, and soon she and another girl concentrated on learning the moves, ignoring most of the kids.

No sign of Mignon when the bell rang. Vivien felt guilty. The ghost had quickly become her best friend, although she didn't exactly understand how or why. They'd begun spending time together, talking about many things and enjoying each other's company. Last night's trick made it hard not to be mad at her. What if someone in her family had seen? Well, Mama might still be able to do that much.

Vivien would love to tell Mama about Mignon, her first best friend. Or, at least what she knew. Not very much, actually. Mama worried sometimes that she didn't have many friends. Maybe she guessed the cockade pendant came from the ghost, for she hadn't mentioned it since that one time. When Mignon asked why she didn't wear it, Vivien admitted Mama had seen it, and she was afraid to let her see it again.

With their getting home first on the bus route, Vivien and Lauren had time to read or do homework. They'd reached the end of January, and a few days of warmer weather surprised everyone. Vivien took a lawn chair to the back yard and settled in with another book on French history. This one gave more details of the French revolution, also called The Reign of Terror. She'd just read a footnote about the book, *The Scarlet Pimpernel,* and made a note of it in the notebook she often carried.

"It's an interesting book."

Vivien looked up and shaded her eyes with her hand. "You've read it?"

"A long time ago."

Mignon looked pretty in a pink dress with a short capelet

around her shoulders. Most of the ghosts Vivien had met wore the same clothes all the time.

"I'm sorry about what I did last night. I only meant to tease."

"It was a shock."

"I know. I won't do it again."

Vivien made her promise no more teasing or sudden appearances with other people around. She reached to set the notebook on the wall of the well, then noticed a slug making a trail of slime. She laid it in her lap instead.

"You've never told me when you lived, what sort of life you lived. You must have had lots of pretty clothes."

"Oh, yes." Mignon whirled around, the full skirt spreading out around her. "*Maman* made some of my clothes. We went shopping so often."

"Where did you live?"

"Paris. Such a beautiful city."

"What did you father do?"

"Isn't it such a beautiful afternoon?" She whirled again. "It's called false spring."

"Why won't you tell me about yourself?"

"There isn't much to tell. I don't ask about you."

"You seem to already know a lot about me."

Vivien heard the sound of the back fence being pulled away from the corner of the shed. She turned in the chair and saw the old Gypsy woman squeeze through the opening.

Mignon disappeared.

Vivien stood. "What do you want?" The interruption irritated her because Mignon seemed about to reveal her past.

The woman walked toward her and made a sign with her hand. She gave Vivien a smile, which made her look younger.

"You wear the talisman. Good."

Vivien's hand went to it automatically. The woman looked up at the kitchen window. Vivien followed her gaze, thinking her mother might be looking out. She could only see the ceiling of the room.

"The girl is not your friend."

"How do you know?" Vivien spoke softly, although she wanted to shout at the woman. In spite of some of the things Mignon did, she liked her. She was her friend. If only she knew more about her.

"Please be careful with her. Do not let her get too close. She . . . she sucks the life out of others."

"What do you mean?" She'd heard the same thing about the ghost on the *Randall* when they were at sea.

"Vivien, come inside and bring the chair. Your daddy will be home soon." Mama stood on the stoop with her apron over her old skirt and sweater. She frowned at seeing the Gypsy.

The woman closed her eyes, and a sad look came over her face. "Do not trust the girl." She retraced her steps to the fence and slipped through. Vivien stood and folded the chair. When she reached the front door, she looked from the high stoop toward the field behind the fence and watched the woman walking up the hill. She hadn't noticed the Gypsies had camped there again. The sun, low in the west, reflected off the windshield of the pickup truck.

"What did she want?" Mama asked.

Instead of avoiding answering, Vivien said, "She warned me about the ghost."

"I see. Is she a threat? The ghost I mean."

"No, not yet." Vivien knew Mama worried about her safety and wished she could tell her everything, but Mama had said she couldn't help her in any of these encounters.

The sound of the car pulling in through the gate cut short

their conversation. Vivien put away the lawn chair and helped set the table.

Should she trust Mignon or the old Gypsy woman? Neither? A warning also came from the woman in the store. Did Mignon present some sort of danger?

THIRTEEN

The next school trip took the older students to the Limoges porcelain factory, which made expensive dishes and elaborate pieces of porcelain. They toured the factory, stopping to watch each process. The women working the line gave kids an unfinished cup, plate, or saucer, until a supervisor stopped them. Afterward, they chipped a plate or broke off a cup handle to give to the rest of the kids. Vivien had gotten an undamaged dinner plate, fired, not glazed. Still, she treasured it and slipped it into the school bag she'd brought with her.

After the tour, the guide led them into a gift shop, where they could buy finished items. If they could afford it. Vivien found a small porcelain box with a very French scene, probably 18th century design. The price was far above the money she'd brought with her.

After the factory visit, they had half an hour to visit shops in the neighborhood before lunch. Vivien spied a bookstore down the street and headed for it. Before she reached her goal, Mignon appeared.

"They will all be in French, you know," she said.

"*Oui, je comprends.*"

"You do not *comprends* enough." Mignon laughed.

"I know. I just want to see what sort of books they have."

"Dusty old ones that will make you sneeze."

Vivien laughed. "Probably."

They walked arm-in-arm through the door, setting a bell off. It jangled again when they closed the door. Mignon wandered off. Vivien stood looking in awe at the rows of bookcases, with shelves filled to the edges. The store had been there a long time. Dust whirled in the sunlight coming through the front windows. The wood floor creaked with every step. In the window and toward the front of the store, most shelves held modern, current books, both fiction and non-fiction. Children's books sat on shelves to the right side.

On a glass counter to the right sat a very old, brass cash register, heavily decorated with brass filigrees and designs, with five columns of buttons in ten rows. A handle on the right side registered each sale, which appeared behind the glass-sided box on top. On the left side, a round box held a roll of paper on which the receipt would be printed.

"*Bonjour.*" A worn-looking man came from the rear and went behind the counter. He looked older than her parents, not as old as her grandma. "*Comment puis-je vous aider?*"

"Uh . . ." Vivien tried to remember how to say, "I'm just looking." The words wouldn't come. Suddenly, Mignon stood beside her. "*Je regarde juste,*" she whispered in Vivien's ear. Vivien repeated the words.

The man harumphed. "*Tu es americaine.*"

"*Oui.*" She went to the counter. "*Avez-vous Jules Verne?*" The first French author's name she could think of at that moment.

The man came out from behind the counter and led her to a bookcase against the opposite wall. He pulled a large volume from a high shelf and handed it to her. *L'Ile Mysterieuse.*

She guessed it to be the same size as a sheet out of her writing tablet for school, about 8½" by 11". The binding appeared to be tooled leather, dyed red, with gold accents. A picture of a hot air balloon had been painted in a tooled gilt frame. She tried to turn the pages, but it was too heavy to open and look through. She went to the counter and set it down very carefully opening the front cover. The price of 10,000 francs had been penciled on the corner of the first blank page.

Facing the title page was a fanciful illustration of the coast of a tropical area with a ship foundering. The date 1923 had been printed at the bottom of the page.

She calculated in her head: 10,000 francs equaled about $20. She reached into the pocket of her jacket and grasped the colorful French bills plus several coins, her savings over the past year. When they arrived in France, their American dollars and cents had to be converted to military scrip, all small paper bills, or French francs. She'd only brought French money with her since the scrip couldn't be used off post.

She made a show of putting the money on the counter and counting it out. It amounted to 8,500 francs, plus a few small coins. *"Je suis desolé."*

The old man looked from her to the money and shrugged. He returned to reading a newspaper, although she noticed him glance at her over it.

She shrugged in turn and walked toward the door, leaving the book on the counter. Daddy had said more than once that the French people were eager to get hold of American money. If she had real money, greenbacks, the old man might be eager to have that, but it was illegal to spend in the French market.

She shuffled toward the door, looking as desolate as she

could. Behind her, the man cleared his throat. "Eight thousand francs?" he said in a heavy accent.

"Seventy-five?" She turned to face him and moved back toward the counter. "Leaves me two hundred francs for my lunch."

He hesitated, mumbled a few words in French. She put the money on the counter again. He picked up the 7,500 in bills. "*C'est bien?*" she asked.

"*Oui. Merci.*"

He rang up the purchase on the cash register and handed her the receipt. She slipped it into the book and walked outside, holding her new treasure against her chest. The other kids had already gathered at the bus, and she hurried to catch up. Mignon walked beside her.

"You could have bought a pretty piece of jewelry or anything nicer in one of the other stores," Mignon said. "Why the dusty old book?"

Usually, Vivien would have made excuses to justify her choice. However, this choice needed no explanation. "I bought it because I wanted it," she said.

"*Bien,*" Mignon said and faded from sight.

Why didn't her friend understand the wonder of books? Her interests lay in nice clothes and shoes. She loved jewelry and purses. Once in a while, Vivien envied her flair for fashion. Most of the time, Vivien wore jeans and oversize shirts if she could. She couldn't dress that way on post. Especially not in school. Girls and women had to wear skirts or dresses when they bowled and shopped or ate at the cafeteria.

The teacher let her take the book onto the bus and put it in her satchel with the plate before everyone headed down the street to a small café. Mr. Gregerson and Madame Guilbeau warned them when they got too loud. Vivien and several of the kids ordered potato leek soup, which came with slices of baguette and lots of fresh butter. Since they weren't supposed to drink the water, most of the kids got sodas. Vivien and two others got hot tea. Hot drinks were okay.

As it turned out, she didn't have to pay her last francs for lunch. The teachers used money from a fund set up for field trips and other learning experiences.

On the two-hour drive back to Fontenet, Vivien paged through the book, pausing on the illustrations scattered throughout. She tried to read some of the French. Most of it was beyond her ability. She'd just have to work harder with Madame Guilbeau.

The regular buses sat lined up when they reached the school. A few parents came to pick up their kids. Vivien boarded the small Citroen bus with Lauren, whose class didn't get to go on the trip. For a while, Lauren pouted because she didn't get to go to Limoges. After Vivien showed her the book, she happily watched while Vivien turned the pages. By the time they reached home, she also knew everything her big sister had done and seen. Except for Mignon, of course. When they got home, Vivien gave her the plate.

"It's not very pretty," Lauren said.

"You can paint your own picture on it," Mama said.

Lauren thought it a very good idea and went to look for leftover paints from the paint-by-number pictures she'd done.

"How much did the book cost you?" Mama asked.

She told her. "But it's very old. Probably worth a lot more."

"That's a lot of money, though."

"I know."

"How much of your savings do you have left?"

"Five hundred francs. And ten dollars in scrip."

"Vivien!"

"I'll treasure it forever."

"Don't come asking your father or me for money the next time we go into St. Jean."

"I won't." It hit her then how broke she was. She had spent nearly all of her savings. With an allowance of two hundred francs and fifty cents in scrip a week, it would take several weeks to rebuild her savings. Even so, she didn't regret buying the book.

Daddy scolded her, too, when he got home. However, he sat down at the table after dinner and let her show him the book. Later, she overheard him telling Mama, "It's pretty old and in good shape. It might be worth something someday."

After everyone went to bed, Mignon appeared in the back yard, throwing small bits of gravel at the bedroom window again. She hadn't appeared late at night for a while, so Vivien didn't get mad. She crawled out of bed and, putting on the robe over her nightgown and the warm carpet slippers, she slipped out of the house.

They talked about the fun they had on the trip. "Thanks for letting me go with you," Mignon said.

"I couldn't stop you if I wanted."

"If you told me not to go, I wouldn't."

"Well, there may be times . . ."

"I got you something." Mignon reached into the pocket of her jacket and drew out a box.

Vivien opened it. Inside was a gold ring with a faceted red stone.

"Oh, it's beautiful."

"It's a ruby. It was my mother's."

"Your mother's? I can't keep it. You need to have it. Besides, it looks expensive."

"I want you to have it. I have lots more jewelry that belonged to her. Put it on."

Vivien slipped it on the ring finger of her left hand. Too big for that finger, she found it fit the middle finger perfectly. It was pretty and she wanted to accept the gift but feared she would feel guilty later on.

"Really, I can't."

"Tell you what. You wear it for a while. If I decide I should keep it, I will ask for it back."

"I'm not even sure I can wear it. Mama will see it."

"Don't put it on until you leave the house. No one in school will notice."

She could wear it once in a while, Vivien decided. Then, she thought of the French cockade still in the little box in her dresser. She wore it only that once.

FOURTEEN

February arrived with another cold spell. The first couple of days, it rained off and on. The bus and the classroom felt colder than ever. Vivien sometimes wore the cockade pendant and the ruby ring at school. She changed from the talisman on the bus in the morning and put on the gifts from Mignon. Madame Guilbeau admired the cockade, and thankfully, no one else noticed it or the ring.

Vivien visited the church on Sunday afternoons. Mignon joined her, and Vivien felt happy to see her. She wished Mignon could be at the party for her birthday next month since she would turn thirteen, a real teenager.

She and Lauren spent less time together. Her little sister had met a French girl about her age in the village, and they played together on Saturdays. Her use of French improved, and her friend already knew some English from school, so they had little problem communicating.

Vivien took long walks on nice days, and often Mignon would join her. Before too long, she was familiar with every street in Asnieres. The main street ran north/south through town. Her house sat on the east side of the street. Walking the small number of streets in the village took less than an hour. After a time, the villagers smiled and waved when she walked by. The baker already knew her since it had become her job to fetch fresh baguettes for lunch. Mama had learned to make the potato and leek soup, and the bread tasted so good with it. They fell in love with French bread early on, but a loaf was only good for the one day. The next day, Mama used it for French toast, if any was left. Otherwise, it got too hard to eat.

One Sunday in February, Vivien stood with Mignon in the church, talking about its history and the village. Unlike her first visit, the door was closed when she reached it. Cold filled the sanctuary, and Vivien kept her hands in the pockets of her coat.

The main door opened, and a shaft of light penetrated the gloom. A dark figure cast a shadow on the stone floor. It drew nearer and became Pere Antoine. He frowned and looked around the sanctuary.

"*Bonjour*, Pere Antoine," Vivien said.

"Ah, mademoiselle." He looked confused. "You are alone?"

Mignon had faded away the moment he stepped across the threshold. She'd done that before when people appeared. Vivien wondered why since no one else could see her, or so she thought.

"*Oui.* I am alone."

"Strange. I felt . . ." He smiled and reached to shake hands. "I see you here now, but you do not come to Sunday services."

"No. I'm not Catholic."

"Perhaps if you come, I can convert you." He smiled, yet he still seemed uneasy.

"I don't think Mama would like that."

"Very well. You are always welcome. Is there anything you need?"

"*Non, merci.*"

"I am almost always here if you ever need . . ." He trailed off.

She thanked him again, and he went toward the altar, where he knelt a moment, then disappeared through the door to the left. Had he heard her talking to Mignon? Did he sense Mignon's presence? She remembered he'd acted the same way the first time she'd visited and Mignon appeared. Maybe she imagined his reaction.

Mignon didn't reappear, and after a quarter of an hour, Vivien walked home. Daddy bent under the hood of the car, adjusting something, or replacing spark plugs. She called hello and went inside. She couldn't bring herself to stay and help in the cold.

Over the next two weeks, Vivien and Mignon got together often in spite of the cold weather. Almost every Sunday they met at the church in the village, and they walked together on Saturday afternoons. Sometimes, she found an isolated spot on the playground at school where they could talk without being seen. They had so much to talk about, but rarely did Mignon reveal much about herself.

She asked questions about the States. How did living in one state differ from another? What was the food like? The people? The schools? Where would Vivien move to after France?

Vivien had lived in four states so far, two of them before she started school. She remembered little about them, only what her parents told her.

"Your mother and father were born in different states," Mignon said one day. "How did they meet?" They walked to the swings on the playground.

Vivien told her about her father being stationed in Tennessee, at Camp Forrest, and meeting Mama in Manchester where she worked in a café. "Daddy is from Illinois up north."

"They married in Tennessee?"

"No, Daddy got transferred to Camp Carson in Colorado. Mama went there by train with her sister, and they got married in Colorado Springs. When Daddy shipped out to another camp, Mama went home and stayed with her parents. He visited her in Tennessee before being sent to Europe. I was born during the war while he was in France."

"Oh, he came here before?"

"Yes. He says everything is very different now." Most of the other kids played around the corner or over on the baseball diamond. "Where were you born?"

"La Rochelle."

"That's not far from here." About an hour's drive southwest, on the coast, and where they went to shop in the main PX for that area of France. The main hospital was also there.

Before Vivien could ask more about Mignon's background, the school bell rang. Mignon said, "*Au revoir,*" and faded away quickly. Vivien had found out little about her friend no matter how hard she tried.

The first of March, Mama announced plans for Vivien's big day. Her birthday being on Thursday, they had arranged to hold the party on the following Saturday at the NCO club. Everyone in school would be invited.

"Can we invite the high school kids, too?" Vivien asked. "Some of their little brothers and sisters will be there."

Her parents hesitated to agree because of the added cost. They finally agreed since it was a special birthday.

Mama reworked one of her dark blue skirts, and they bought a light blue sweater in St. Jean. Vivien wanted to wear the cockade pendant and ruby ring, but she didn't want to have to worry about anyone seeing them. She decided to at least wear the ring, and the talisman given to her by the old woman would look good with her new sweater.

Saturday arrived and Mama helped her fix her hair. When Vivien looked in the mirror, she felt so grownup with her hair pinned up in a French twist like a grown woman's. Lauren wanted her hair fixed too, and Mama pulled it back into a ponytail and tied a pretty scarf around the rubber band.

Vivien and family arrived half an hour before the party began so they could set up the dining room of the NCO club like they had for the Christmas dance in the officer's club. Drinks could be ordered at the bar, and no one needed money to play the juke box. Piles of sandwiches and cookies sat on one table. The tables surrounded an open space for dancing, and each table had a small vase of pink flowers.

Vivien couldn't believe her eyes. Everything looked better than she'd expected, as if her parents had suddenly found a cache of money.

Kids began arriving at four o'clock Some of the parents came in with their kids, leaving as soon as they checked things out. Mama and Daddy had asked another couple, friends of theirs, to chaperone. Mr. and Mrs. Jefferson were older, and their children had grown up and left home before he went to France as a civilian employee of the Army. Miss Arnold, the first and second grade teacher, also agreed to come.

Once the party started, Mama and Daddy headed off to the movies. The party was to end at six o'clock. So would the movie.

At first, the kids surrounded the food table and the bar. Soon, they danced to the records playing on the jukebox. With chaperones present, everyone behaved their best. At four-thirty, Mrs. Jefferson announced time to open the presents. A pile of gifts in pretty papers and bows sat on a table near the dance floor. Music continued to play, and Vivien sat on a chair, unwrapping presents. Mrs. Jefferson stood by in case she needed help.

Halfway through the pile, Vivien opened a small box from Richard Swiatek. Inside, she found a chain link bracelet in a gold-toned metal with a heart-shaped charm dangling from it. The charm had been engraved with her name and the date. He helped her put it on and kissed her cheek. Vivien stopped breathing for a moment. She thanked him instead of wrapping her arms around his neck as she wanted to.

The remaining gifts might have seemed like a letdown after that, except Vivien loved opening presents. Half of the excitement lay in seeing what was inside, and whatever it might be, she loved it. She'd saved the one from her sister 'til last, concerned Lauren might be embarrassed by what she'd gotten her. It turned out to be a metal bookmark with a cat figure on the top. She loved it.

When all the presents were opened and all the cards had been gathered up, she thanked everyone for coming and for the gifts. Miss Arnold brought out the cake with lighted candles. She set it on the table for Vivien to blow them out. A girl in the group asked what she wished for. She ignored the question, and with Miss Arnold's help, cut slices to put on small paper plates. After everyone had a slice, Vivien and Mrs. Jefferson put gifts and cards in brown paper grocery bags. The dancing resumed while they worked.

Vivien looked up and watched kids dancing or talking in small groups. Everyone had enjoyed themselves. At that moment, Mignon appeared on the dance floor, standing right behind Richard as he danced with a high school student Vivien didn't know. The ghost reached out and pushed him in the back. He stumbled forward and to his right, pushing his partner to his left. The girl regained her balance and looked angrily at Richard. He spun around, looking to identify the person responsible. Mignon stood glaring at him, but he looked through her. He glared at the kids near him, trying to identify the culprit.

A couple of people laughed. Other dancers shifted away slightly, not wanting him to think they'd done it, some expecting there might be a fight. Vivien went to him, dropping a piece of wrapping paper on the floor.

"Richard, are you okay?"

"Someone pushed me." He glared around at those nearest to him.

"I think you slipped. Maybe on that piece of paper." She bent down and picked it up. He watched her and frowned.

"Someone pushed me," he said again.

Mrs. Jefferson joined them. "I'm sure you slipped," she said. "Either way, it was an accident."

Vivien took his hand. "Dance with me?"

He looked to where his partner had been standing, who had moved away. He nodded and held out his arms. They began and others followed. Vivien saw Mignon standing against the wall near the door, a smirk on her face.

CHAPTER
FIFTEEN

Parents began arriving to pick up the kids a few minutes before six o'clock. The Jeffersons and Miss Arnold gathered up paper plates and cups. The large trash can, already half full of wrapping paper, filled quickly. Mama and Daddy arrived just after six and helped with cleaning up.

They checked around to make sure they hadn't missed anything. The manager of the club left his office and began opening up for the crowd of G.I.s, some of whom waited outside in the cold. He turned off the jukebox they'd continued to play while they worked. Saturday nights, the young soldiers packed the club, drinking, playing the jukebox, some dancing with girlfriends and wives.

Lauren chattered away in the back seat on the way home. She'd danced several times with a boy from her class she liked a lot. She whispered to Vivien that she hoped they would sit together at lunch time. When Mama asked questions about the party, Vivien's anger at Mignon made her responses terse. Yes, she had a wonderful time. Yes, she danced a lot. Everyone gave such wonderful presents. She'd kept the cards where Mrs. Jefferson had written down the gift so she could send thank you notes.

When the questions stopped, she sat silently seething. Mignon had nearly ruined her birthday party. How could she? They were supposed to be friends. Why pick on Richard? She couldn't wait to give her friend a piece of her mind.

Before the party, she'd hoped Mignon might appear. Maybe they could share a moment. Instead, after what the ghost did, she could hardly wait to tell her off.

She turned the ring on her finger in her agitation. Suddenly, she realized she had to take it off so no one saw it. Slipping it into her small purse, she wondered if she would ever wear it again.

It was nearly seven o'clock when they got home. Vivien took cards and presents into the bedroom, saying she wanted to look at everything again. She and Lauren took off their party clothes. Vivien hung up her new clothes carefully. She'd felt so grownup tonight.

When she'd had her first menstrual period back in Breckinridge, she'd been told she had become a woman. The fact she didn't look it bothered her for a while. Mama explained that would come within a few years. After a year and a half, she still didn't look it: girl's figure, thin legs, no bosom. Tonight, though, dressed up and with her hair put up, she felt what she didn't see when looking in a mirror.

And it nearly got ruined by her best friend. Vivien tried hard to hold onto the good feelings she'd had at the party, but anger kept intruding.

Vivien had changed into nightgown and robe and sat on the bed looking through everything. She checked the cards where Mrs. Jefferson wrote down who gave her what. Movement at the window caught her attention. She looked up to see

Mignon's face, glowing against the night's blackness. Vivien turned her back to the window and continued organizing. Mama came in with a box of notecards for her to use as thank you notes.

"You can give most of them out at school Monday," she said. "We'll work on them tomorrow."

Vivien thanked her. She looked over her shoulder briefly. Mignon had gone.

As she lay in bed later that night, Vivien couldn't help watching the window for the ghost to reappear. She went from hoping she did so she could tell her off to thinking she never wanted to see her again.

Her clock cuckooed twice just before she drifted to sleep.

SUNDAY AFTERNOON, Vivien wandered to the church. She half wanted Mignon to come. She sat quietly in a pew and thought about the strange friendship she found herself in.

She'd never had a best friend before. Other kids in school her age liked her, and she liked most of her schoolmates. They all played together, without her being close to any of them. Did best friends act like Mignon? If so, maybe she didn't want one, especially if it meant she couldn't have any other friends.

She especially liked Richard. He was older but never treated her like a kid. She held up her hand and looked at the bracelet. She really liked it and appreciated his giving it to her. He made her feel like an equal. Maybe she'd see him again, but with him away in high school, the odds were against it. She had no clue when he and his family would rotate back to the States and they'd lose contact. Maybe they could start writing letters to each other.

A chill passed through her. Either someone had opened the

door behind her or Mignon had appeared. The someone would probably be Pere Antoine. She liked him and almost hoped he had come in. When she turned around, though, Mignon sat on the pew behind her.

"You are mad at me."

"Yes," Vivien said. "You almost ruined my birthday party."

"I didn't mean to."

"Why did you push Richard?" Vivien glared at the ghost.

Mignon shrugged. "I do not know. He seemed so smug when he kissed your cheek. I got angry."

"I don't belong to you, Mignon."

"I know. But I wish we could be together every day. See each other. Talk about everything."

"I'd like that, too. Sometimes. But I have my family and teachers and other kids in school. If I talk to you when they're around, they'll think I'm crazy."

"I know. But I am lonely."

"Aren't there others like you? Don't you see other ghosts?"

"Only me."

"I saw other ghosts in the department store before Christmas. Don't you know them?"

"I saw them once. They did not like me."

"Why?"

"I do not know. They had a grownup looking after them."

"I'm sorry."

"I have only you. And when you move back to the States, I will have no one."

"I'm sorry."

"Can't you stay?"

"No. We have to go where the Army sends us."

Footsteps sounded on the stone floor from near the altar. Vivien spun in the pew to see Pere Antoine approaching.

"I startled you. I am sorry," he said.

"It's okay. I was deep in thought."

"You speak to yourself when you are deep in thought?" He must have heard her talking with Mignon.

"Sometimes. It's sort of like writing dialog in a story."

He sat on the pew across the aisle, facing her. "I sense . . . something when you are here. Maybe something going on in your life. Are things good at home?"

"Oh, yes. We're very happy here."

"*Bien*. If you are troubled, though, I am here."

"I know." It was the second time he'd offered to help her.

SIXTEEN

Mignon didn't reappear again until Wednesday during morning recess. When she did come, she stood at a distance and waved. Vivien looked up from the usual bench where she practiced French pronunciations. Vivien smiled at the sight of her friend, dressed to the nines in a full skirt in grey felt and a pink sweater. She'd pulled her shoulder-length hair up into a ponytail tied with a bright green scarf. She looked every bit the American teenager.

Mignon walked toward her, and Vivien noticed she wore black patent leather shoes. *No one wears patent leather in winter.*

"Should we go to our corner?" Mignon asked.

"No. I'm practicing reading in French, so no one is paying attention to me if I talk out loud."

"I am sorry about your birthday party."

"It's okay so long as you don't do it again."

"I promise."

"Okay." Vivien picked up the book and pretended to read from it. "Once it gets warmer, we may have to meet outside someplace in the village on Sundays instead of the church."

"Why?"

"I think Pere Antoine suspects you're there."

"He cannot."

"He asked me about talking to myself the last time."

"Ah, I do not know how he would know, but we can find another place."

Vivien saw Arlene, her fellow seventh grader, coming towards her. "I promised to teach her the latest clapping game."

Anger tightened Mignon's expression. "Why? This is our time."

"I didn't know if you would come. Besides, you promised not to get angry about my other friends."

"Sorry." Mignon looked down at the ground.

"Can you show me now?" Arlene asked.

Mignon looked up at her classmate with such a look of spite, Vivien felt frightened, then disappeared.

Once she got home that afternoon, Vivien checked to see if the Gypsies still camped on the hill. She changed clothes and grabbed the French textbook.

"I'm going outside and recite conjugations," she told her mother.

Mama looked up from the meat loaf almost ready to go into the oven. "Okay. Don't go far."

"I won't."

She slipped through the gap between the fence and shed and headed up the hill. When she got close to the caravans, one of the women sat near the fire, probably fixing dinner. Vivien approached the old woman's caravan.

"You are worried," the woman said when she sat down in the lawn chair. She motioned for Vivien to sit beside her in the other.

"You know about the ghost," Vivien began.

The woman nodded.

"You tried to warn me about her. She's beginning to frighten me."

"How?"

"She doesn't like my other friends."

"She has hurt someone?"

"No, not yet. But she gets mad if I pay attention to them. She pushed a boy the other night. He gave me a birthday present and kissed me on the cheek."

"She wishes not to share you."

"Will she start hurting people?"

"She has given to you something?"

How did she know? "A pendant and a ring."

"You must give them back."

"What if she won't take them? She acts like I've hurt her feelings if I don't wear them."

"You still wear the talisman." She pointed at it hanging from the cord around Vivien's neck. "Do not take it off. If you have worn the others . . ."

"I have."

"She has some power over you. Offer them back to her. If she will not accept, put them in a metal box. Around it, tie a silver chain."

"I have a tin box, but I don't have a silver chain."

"Angelette," the woman called out. A young girl, about Lauren's age came running. The woman spoke to her in the same language she'd used when she first came to the house. The girl nodded and went into the caravan. In a moment she reappeared and handed the woman a very old metal box, about the size of a cardboard cigar box. The woman opened it. She searched through several pieces of jewelry until she found what she wanted. She raised her hand and held a chain between forefinger and thumb.

A small silver cross hung from it. She started to undo the catch. She changed her mind and handed both to Vivien. "I would like them back."

"Sure. When?"

"You will know when you no longer need them."

"Thank you. Will the cross help?"

The woman nodded and got up. "We can hope." At the door of her caravan, she turned back, nodded again, and went inside.

That night, Vivien worried about giving back the pendant and ring. When should she do it? How? She pictured Mignon getting angry, accusing her of not liking her anymore. There must be something she could say to make it easier.

She lay in bed trying to come up with reasons. Finally, she thought, *I will be returning to the States next year. If I give them back to her now, I won't forget next year.*

She determined to tell her Sunday when they visited the church. Going there had become a habit, and although she'd talked about finding a different place to meet, she didn't want to give up the feeling of peace, especially before Mignon showed up or those times she didn't show up at all.

She liked Pere Antoine, too. Maybe one day they could have a longer conversation. She hadn't been saved by accepting Jesus as her savior in Grandma's church. Several times, she'd almost answered the call, but it made her uncomfortable, which she'd never tell Mama or Grandma. She liked the trappings of Catholic churches, the ceremonies she'd seen from a distance. Maybe Pere Antoine could give some insight into what Catholicism was all about.

Mignon didn't show up at school the next day and Vivien breathed a sigh of relief. However, putting off what might be an unpleasant confrontation made her tense and snappish. Yet, she would put it off forever if she could.

Friday, Daddy announced he had to go on TDY to Germany again for a whole week the beginning of April. He'd arranged transportation so he could leave the car for Mama to do the shopping. The "girls" planned what they would do while on their own. It would be the same as when they lived in Tennessee. As much as they loved their father, Vivien and Lauren looked forward to having Mama to themselves for a while.

It rained most of Saturday. The weather had been warming, anticipating spring. A few trees budded out around the village and on the grounds around school. Bulbs began sending shoots above ground. What was France like in spring?

What if it rained Sunday, and Vivien couldn't go to the church? Now, delaying the moment didn't bring such a feeling of relief. However, Sunday dawned fresh, and the sun chased away early morning clouds.

Of course, having a nice day didn't chase away her fears.

That morning, the four of them sprawled over the living room, reading the papers, after breakfast. Vivien worked on the crossword puzzle. She'd gotten only a little better, but she kept trying.

Lauren's friend, Estelle, arrived to play. She'd not been able to come Saturday, but their parents agreed she could come over Sunday after church.

Vivien announced she was going for a walk. Mama looked up and told her to be careful. Daddy nodded. Lauren and Estelle were in the bedroom and couldn't care less. With the sun shining brightly, the day had warmed, and she only needed a sweater to ward off the chill. She arrived at the church about the usual time and sat in a pew near the middle where she could see most of the sanctuary.

When alone, she usually didn't think about anything specific, letting her thoughts whirl round in her head. Today, however, she had a mission, and she wanted to keep focused. She put her hand around the tin box in her pocket and worried about her ghost friend's reaction to her returning the tokens. Mignon had made clear her desire to be Vivien's one and only friend. She resented time Vivien spent with others. Vivien had never had a best friend before, but this wasn't the friendship Vivien wanted.

SEVENTEEN

Vivien reached into the pocket of her jeans. The metal of the chain and the ring felt cool to her fingers. A rush of cold air made her turn toward the outer door. Did Mignon bring the cold air with her presence or by simply opening the door?

The ghost slid into the pew beside her. "You are late." Mignon often didn't appear until Vivien had arrived.

"I wasn't sure I wanted to come." Vivien had waited until the last minute to leave the house.

"I told you I am sorry, and it will not happen again."

"I know."

"You are my friend. I need to see you."

"That's the problem."

"What problem?

"You want me all to yourself. You're my best friend, but not my only friend. You can't do some things and my other friends can."

"Like what?" Mignon sounded angry.

"If anyone saw me playing games with you—"

"It is not my fault!"

"I know. But we can't change . . . You aren't of this world."

"I am here, am I not?"

"Yes, but you shouldn't be."

Mignon stared at her, a stricken look on her face. "Where should I be?"

Vivien swallowed hard and looked away. She hadn't meant to ever say anything about Mignon not having found peace. Why did she still wander the Earth trying to find a friend?

"Because I am dead." Mignon said the word they both avoided as long as they could. She was dead, but still wandered the world looking for something she must not have had in life. A friend? Love?

"Why aren't you at peace?" Vivien had heard those words used to describe the dead, but she'd already found several ghosts not at peace. She'd found out why. Why wasn't Mignon at peace?

"At peace? I am too young to be at peace. I want to be alive." She turned to face Vivien squarely. "You make me feel alive. You are my friend."

"But I will be gone next year. What will you do then?"

"I will come with you."

"Can you do that?" The possibility both surprised and frightened her.

Mignon sighed and her shoulders slumped. "*Non. Je suis au piège ici.*"

"You are . . ."

"Trapped here. This is where I died."

"Asnieres?"

"*Oui.*"

"You can't leave this area?"

"*Non.*"

"I'm sorry, Mignon." Pity for the girl overwhelmed Vivien. A girl her own age, dead, unable to find peace. So terribly sad.

"How did you die?"

Mignon stiffened. "I do not remember."

"You must—"

"*Non.*"

"Please, Mignon. I want to help, but I can't unless I know more."

"I do not need help. I need your friendship. The priest comes. I must go."

The door to the left of the altar opened and the priest came through. He smiled on seeing Vivien.

"*Bienvenue.*" He came toward her. "How are you?"

"Good. And you?"

"Very well, *merci.*"

He sat down across from her. Ever since they met, she'd been trying to figure out Pere Antoine's age. When tired, he looked at least fifty. Today, he seemed full of energy, eyes sparkling, his smile warm, and looked no more than thirty-five.

It occurred to her the priest might know about Mignon. She didn't know when her friend died so had no idea if he might have been in Asnieres at the time.

"Pere Antoine, I wondered . . ."

"*Oui.*"

"Have you ever heard of a girl who died here in Asnieres? About my age. Her name is Mignon Cuvier."

He thought a moment. "I do not remember that name. When did she die?"

"I don't know."

"How did you hear of her?"

"Someone told me her name and thought she died here."

He studied her face, his own expression quizzical. He

looked about to ask more, but with a slight shake of his head, said, "If you like, I could look through the church records for that name. There could be more information there."

"Would you? I'd really appreciate it."

"Of course. Anything else you would like for me to do?"

"Oh, no. If you find something . . . I mean, can I come back next Sunday and see if you found anything?"

"I am not sure it would be so quickly, but we can at least talk about it then."

"Thank you. Thank you."

Vivien got up to leave, and Pere Antoine stood to watch her go. She started toward the door but turned and gave the priest a hug. He laughed in surprise.

PERE ANTOINE WORRIED he might not be able to find the information young Vivien seemed so desperate for. Ever since the girl first appeared in the church, he'd wondered what she wanted or needed.

She'd been seen in the Gypsy camp visiting with Hester, the matriarch. He had no problem with Gypsies. In fact, he found them very devoted Catholics. But many of the villagers didn't like them camping in the area, and seeing the American girl visiting the camp made them suspicious of her. Everyone expressed curiosity about her family, and some believed the younger sister's being friends with Estelle Benoit would make it possible to find out more.

He hoped, by finding out about Mignon Cuvier, he might also learn more about Vivien and her family. Of course, they would live in Asnieres only about two years, so it couldn't make much difference in the overall scheme of things. But at the end of their stay, another American family would move into the house. Jerome Lucas did prefer renting to Americans.

Pere Antoine went about the usual Sunday routine. He checked the donation box for the poor, checked supplies and whether any candles needed to be replaced. All the while, he thought about Vivien. He'd come to like her, although they hadn't had much in the way of conversation. Perhaps with this new connection, he'd learn more.

EIGHTEEN

Vivien leaned back against the wall of the school building and felt the sun on her face. Spring flowers would soon bloom, and trees would bud. In fact, some had already begun. The days warmed steadily, and everyone felt and acted more cheerful. At the moment, kids ran and called out to each other in the playground. Samantha had asked her to play clapping games with her, but she expected Lauren to arrive at any time.

A week had passed, and she'd seen the priest on Sunday, but he had nothing to tell her. It had been a busy week, he said, and he'd hardly had time to locate all of the records. He promised to work on the task this week and hoped to have information for her this Sunday.

Everything else in her life moved along. She'd been disappointed when turning thirteen didn't make much difference in her looks but had reconciled to still being treated like a child. She and Mama had a long talk about the changes occurring in her body. The biggest change in recent weeks? Her breasts had begun to swell slightly. At first it delighted her to see her figure become more womanly. Yet, the reflection in the mirror still didn't show much else of her new maturity.

Mama talked about getting her a training bra soon. The thought of wearing a bra both delighted and frightened her. She imagined boys staring at her chest. They wouldn't, of course, since she hadn't much to see there. Lauren became fascinated by the changes, and Vivien tried not to be naked in front of her sister.

Mignon's sudden appearance beside her startled Vivien out of her reverie.

"I startled you?"

"Yeah. I was wool gathering."

"Wool gathering?"

"Yeah, thinking deep thoughts."

"Sorry I interrupted."

"It's okay. I can't visit long. My sister asked me to help her with her French."

"But this is our time together."

"I know, but she's having trouble and needs my help."

"But I need your help, too. And you promised."

"I didn't promise to meet with you today."

"*Non*, but we always meet at this time."

"I know. And I'm sorry. She only asked me at lunch time if I'd help her."

Mignon crossed her arms and pouted. "You love her more than you do me."

"Maybe a little. She is my sister, and I've known her longer than I've known you."

"But I am your best friend."

"Yes, but—"

"You want me to go away."

"Just today. We can talk tonight."

"*Non.* I will not be in your yard tonight." She frowned when Lauren came around the corner of the building.

"There she is, your sweet little sister." Mignon sounded spiteful. She disappeared without another word.

Vivien barely responded when Lauren greeted her. The look Mignon gave her sister worried her. She didn't think Mignon would do anything to hurt Lauren, but the ghost had shown she could be unpredictable.

"You all right?" Lauren asked.

"Yeah. Yes. I'm fine."

Lauren sat next to her and opened her French textbook. Vivien mentally shook herself and tried to concentrate on French and Lauren's questions.

"It's irregular verbs," Lauren said.

"Well, they're irregular. You have to memorize how they're conjugated. You do know what conjugation means?"

"Sure. I am, you are—"

"Right. Regular verbs are conjugated the same, with the same endings." She turned to the first page in the textbook dealing with irregular verbs. "If you repeat irregular verbs over and over, you soon learn them."

She picked *avoir*, one of the first verbs in the book, and told Lauren to conjugate it. Lauren stumbled and Vivien said it aloud: "*J'ai*, I have." Lauren repeated it. Vivien read out the rest and Lauren repeated. All the while, Vivien watched for Mignon to reappear.

When the bell rang, Vivien had become engrossed in saying the words and helping Lauren repeat them. She'd forgotten about Mignon. But when Lauren left for class in the next building, Mignon appeared and followed her.

Vivien's heart skipped a beat. She wanted to follow her sister and the ghost. Surely Mignon would not harm Lauren. She had to know nothing would make Vivien angrier.

Convincing herself that Lauren must be safe, Vivien went on to her own classroom, only to worry all through history class, doubting her decision. When they boarded the little bus at the end of the day, Lauren was perfectly all right.

For a while, Vivien wished she'd done as she intended that Sunday when she meant to return the gifts. Maybe the priest would have some useful information for her this Sunday. Whether he did or didn't, she needed to break off with Mignon. She didn't want to worry about any harm coming to her sister, so she must end the friendship, the sooner the better.

Mignon surprised her and came that night, acting as if nothing had happened. While they sat on the rim of the well, she chatted about lots of things but uttered not one word about Lauren. Nor did she reveal anything of her life or family.

Vivien was not mollified by her supposed best friend's ignoring what had seemed a threat. Nor did she challenge her about it, fearing that doing so might provoke her.

While they talked, Vivien thought about returning the jewelry. She'd decided the church was the place to give them back. However, she'd felt sorry for the girl and didn't do it. Maybe it had more to do with liking Mignon most of the time and enjoying her company. It had to be done and the church would be the best place. She might not be religious, but Vivien believed churches were safe places.

Here, tonight, she worried about Mignon being near to her family. She took hold of the talisman hanging on the cord around her neck. For the first time, it grew warm to the touch.

NINETEEN

Sunday, when Vivien went to the church, she sat on a pew on the left side, rather than the right, as she usually did. The view wasn't all that different, except she could see into the small altar in the niche.

"*Bonjour*, Vivien." Mignon sat in the pew in front of Vivien.

"*Bonjour*."

Mignon wore a short-sleeved, white sweater with a furry, pink collar. The wine-colored full skirt went wonderfully with the sweater. Vivien envied Mignon's clothes more and more. Her family couldn't afford nice things nor so many skirts and sweaters. How did Mignon come by them?

"What do you do when you're not with me?" Vivien asked. She'd wondered for a while. Did she visit others? Sleep? Wander about?

"Nothing."

"How can you do nothing?"

"Time isn't the same for me." Mignon got up and whirled around. "When I want to do something, I do it. Sometimes I watch and listen."

"You watch me?"

"Sometimes."

"Don't do that." Vivien turned away. Had Mignon heard her talking with Pere Antoine? Did she overhear conversations with her family? Or Hester, the gypsy woman?

"Why not?"

"Because it's spying. It's creepy."

"Well, actually, I cannot often. I get glimpses, like looking through a crack in a door."

"Most people don't wander around, you know. Not after . . ."

"They die?" Mignon finished the sentence.

"Well, yeah."

"Those people give up. I will not."

"Don't you want to see your parents again? In the afterlife, I mean."

"Pft. Why would I want to see them again?" Mignon stood. "I will light a candle for them."

Mignon approached the candles displayed on the stand to the right of the altar, a couple of them alight. Most had burned at least half-way down, the melted wax forming solid puddles around the bases. She tried to pick up the long taper used to light the smaller candles but couldn't take hold of it.

"Here, let me." Vivien held the taper to one already burning, and the wick blazed. She tried to hand the taper to Mignon, but she still couldn't hold it. Why couldn't she take hold of it? She had no trouble touching other things. Vivien lit one of the small candles and blew out the taper. "There."

"It does not mean anything."

"But you wanted to do it."

Mignon shrugged. She flounced down the aisle between pews. "How do you like my new clothes?"

"They're very nice."

The ghost stopped and looked around the sanctuary. "Why do you come here?"

"I don't know. It's quiet and peaceful. I can think. And it's a good place for us to meet."

"We need to meet in a place less . . . religious."

"Where?"

"I do not know. I will find a place and tell you at school." Mignon turned thoughtful, looking down with hands together as if praying. "Please promise you will never leave me." Tears glinted in her eyes.

"I can't stay with you forever, Mignon. You must understand. I will grow up. I'll get older. You won't. You will always be a little girl."

"Not if . . ."

"What?" Surely Mignon didn't believe she could some back to life. The only way Vivien wouldn't grow up was if she died. Vivien wrapped her fingers around the amulet. The stones again felt warm. "Mignon, do you want me to die? To be like you?"

"We could be together forever. We would be happy. It is not so bad."

"I don't want to die. There's so much—"

"We could do everything you want to do. Together."

"Except travel. Return to the States to see my grandma. Get married someday." She rarely thought about getting married, but the prospect came to her at that moment. "Together, we could do almost nothing compared to what I want to do. I couldn't hug Mama and Lauren."

"You could. They would not know it, but . . ."

"It's not the same. No, I won't die for you."

"I can make it happen."

"I don't think so. And if you did, I would hate you. We wouldn't be friends anymore."

"Do not say that. I need you to be my friend."

Vivien empathized with the need for a friend. She'd spent most of her young life surrounded by strangers her own age, younger, older, but with whom she rarely connected. She and Mignon could be connected forever. She would never be without a friend.

The amulet thrummed, grew warmer, seeming to hold her back from an abyss.

"Please, Vivien."

"No, I will not die for you."

"No, I do not want you to die. I only want—The priest." She faded.

Pere Antoine appeared through the usual doorway. His face lit up in a smile when he saw Vivien. "I thought to find you here."

"*Bonjour.*"

"*Ça va?*"

"*Ça va.*"

"Good. Good. I have some information for you about the girl, Mignon Cuvier." He reached under his cassock and pulled out a piece of paper. "I doubt you can read my writing. No one can. Sometimes not even I can."

He unfolded the paper and produced a pair of glasses. "The child died in Asnieres in 1937. She was an orphan, or perhaps her mother gave her up. She's buried in the cemetery *au nord de . . .*"

"To the north?"

"*Oui.* In *terrain non consacré.* Unconsecrated ground. She was not a proper *catholique* as she was never christened. And her mother . . ." He blushed. "Perhaps I should not . . ."

Several words popped into Vivien's head. Witch, heathen, pagan. "A prostitute?"

"*Oui, une prostituée.* How do you know this word?"

"I read a lot, Father."

"And you know what it means?"

"*Oui.*" She blushed at the admission. She couldn't remember in what book she'd first encountered the word and the type of woman. Probably in one of Mama's Book-of-the-Month club editions. Mama hadn't approved, one of the few times she'd expressed an opinion about what Vivien read.

"Mignon was born in La Rochelle, placed into an orphanage there, and eventually a family from here adopted her."

"A family named 'Cuvier'?"

"*Non.* Cuvier is her birth name."

"So, you don't know the name of the family who adopted her."

"Sorry, *non.* It may be in the records somewhere, *mais*—but —I have not yet seen their name."

"What did she die of?"

The priest looked down at the paper. "I think it was pneumonia, but what it says in our record is not . . . um . . . *officielle.*"

"Official."

"*Oui.*"

They discussed the information for a few minutes. Pere Antoine tried his best to get her to say why she wanted to find the information, or how she even knew the name. She feared he would think badly of her if she said she knew the girl as a ghost. He probably wouldn't believe her. In her experience, most religious people didn't care for supernatural phenomena.

She asked if she could have the paper, and he handed it to her. He'd written in French, of course, and used some sort of shorthand. The words she could read would jog her memory of their conversation since she intended to write out in English what she'd been told.

What good would it do, knowing what the father found?

That Mignon was a sad person didn't help much. Knowing her mother may have given her up didn't either. Except it must have to do with her remaining attached to this world when she should be at rest in the next.

Maybe Mignon never had friends in her life and sought them out now. Maybe she looked for her mother or a mother figure.

She asked herself these questions over and over when she walked home. She barely noticed the clouds that had gathered while she was inside. However, the wind that blew up when she'd gotten halfway home got her attention.

She reached the gate at her house and stopped to look up at the sky. Could there be a chance of snow at the end of March?

When she got inside, she found Daddy asleep in his chair in the living room. Lauren lay on the sofa reading. Mama sat at the kitchen table, peeling potatoes.

"Have a nice walk?" Mama asked.

"Yeah. It's getting colder, and I think it might snow. Maybe we won't have to go to school tomorrow."

"I don't think they've ever cancelled school because of bad weather."

Vivien joined her mother at the table. "Mashed or fried?" Mama asked.

"Mashed."

Mama handed her the paring knife and she cut the potatoes in small cubes so they would boil up quickly, dropping the pieces into the colander to be rinsed.

"You have found your ghost." It wasn't a question.

"Yes."

"The Gypsy woman is concerned about it?"

"Yes."

"Can you tell me anything about it?"

"Not yet." She finished cutting up a potato and stopped. "I

can't figure out what this one needs. I know what she wants, and the two aren't the same thing."

"Well, if I can help." They both knew there wasn't much she could do. Each generation had one daughter who had the ability to see ghosts and help them while she was young. She had to cope on her own. Why, it seemed no one knew, except the restriction passed down to each daughter and grand-daughter.

Mama picked up the colander and set it under running water. Vivien gathered the peels and dropped them in the slop bucket set against the stove. Mama used it to take all food waste outside to dump in the well.

By the time Mama called everyone to dinner, it had started to snow. Vivien looked out of the window behind Lauren. Snowflakes on the other side of the glass reflected the light from the kitchen. Up the hill, lights glowed from the Gypsy camp. Vivien thought about visiting the old woman again. With more information about Mignon, maybe she could help decide what to do.

Was it safe to talk with her about the ghost when she couldn't talk to Mama? Why would it be different? She'd considered talking with Pere Antoine, but his being a priest might make him doubt what she told him.

Sometimes dealing with these situations alone felt too much of a burden.

TWENTY

Mignon stayed on her best behavior the next few days. Their visits were shorter, and Vivien couldn't help being suspicious. When they did meet, the ghost spoke more and more of finding another place for them. In a few days, she began offering suggestions. After the fourth suggestion, Vivien realized they were all isolated places. No other people nearby, even around the corner or across the street.

One was a shed on the back road between Asnières and Fontenet. No one used it or went there. Or an old barn at the east edge of the village, also unused and isolated. An abandoned house on the north edge.

"When the weather is nice, we could meet in the cemetery. No one goes there except when they bury someone."

She didn't ask Vivien to decide among them, saying she mentioned them only as suggestions. There must be other places.

The next Sunday, Vivien made a point to ask Mignon to meet at the church as usual. "Pere Antoine told me he will be busy that Sunday, but the church will be open as always. We won't be interrupted."

"*D'accord*," Mignon said. "But next time, we must go somewhere else."

The end of March neared. The snow from early in the week had disappeared within a day's time, and the weather turned warm. Madame Guilbeau told Vivien April would see more flowers blooming and trees leafing out. Meanwhile, the kids longed for summer vacation, which couldn't be far behind. Did French kids get a summer vacation? Surely, they did.

Daffodils bloomed around the post gate pillars, with the sign announcing: US Army: Fontenet—Sub-Post. A couple of bushes in their own yard looked about to burst forth in color in front of and behind the house. Everyone seemed more lighthearted. Madame Guilbeau nearly smiled on Friday when Vivien answered a question in a complete sentence. Not only complete, but the response was also a particularly tricky one for a person who hadn't spoken French her whole life.

The French teacher returned to her office a little earlier than usual to finish up some paperwork before the weekend. Vivien felt almost giddy after the praise she'd received.

Mignon appeared beside her on the bench. "I think I've found the perfect place."

"Mignon, I'm perfectly happy with meeting in the church. It's close to home, out of the weather . . ." Although they were often alone there on Sundays, at least for a while, she felt it to be a safer place.

"But the pesky priest keeps interrupting. We never know how much time we'll have."

"We have those nights when you come to the house, our time here at school."

"It's always with someone else around. We want to be careful."

"That's what life is all about. People. Families. Friends."

"*Oui*, but as you said, I am not alive. We either must both be alive or—"

"No!" Vivien slammed the book closed. Kids playing nearby looked over with puzzled expressions. She lay the book back down in her lap, pretending she'd reacted to a problem with her studies.

Mignon, startled by the tone of voice, looked shocked. She disappeared without another word.

"Sunday," Vivien whispered to herself. "I have to end this on Sunday."

She worried about seeing Mignon again and found it hard to concentrate in class. Friday passed quickly, and the family planned to go into St. Jean to do some shopping on Saturday. Summer would soon arrive, and Lauren had nearly grown out of a couple of her dresses while Vivien needed a new pair of shoes. Bad weather had been predicted and they decided it would be safer to try Les Galleries.

After lunch on Saturday, they all got into the car and headed north to St. Jean. Daddy parked on the street down from the department store. They'd found that, if they shopped carefully, some things could be bought more cheaply on the French market than in the big PX in La Rochelle. Plus, they didn't have to drive so far. The girls also enjoyed the comparative freedom. In the department store, they could wear their jeans. In the PX, if they didn't have dresses on, they couldn't buy anything. They often complained about the Army's strict rules on how women and girls must dress.

They found a dress for Lauren, and Vivien picked out a pair of white buck shoes. Their parents wanted a couple of throw rugs for the floor in their bedroom, and they told the girls to look around on their own but to be near the front doors in twenty minutes. Lauren went off to the gift counter, where they sold trinkets like jewelry boxes and perfume bottles. Vivien made her way to the jewelry counter.

She wandered the length of one counter until it made a right turn. Several styles of bracelets caught her eye, but none seemed to her as pretty as the one Richard gave her. A ruby ring reminded her of the one still in the box with the cockade.

"Lovely, isn't it?"

Vivien looked up and recognized the same woman—or ghost—she'd met there before.

"Yes, it is." She looked around. No one else stood at the counters or in the general area.

"You still wear the amulet."

"Yes."

"*Bon*. You will need it in the coming days."

"Why? What's going to happen?"

"You've learned that friends aren't always what they seem. Don't misplace your trust." Again, a host of smaller figures appeared behind her.

"What should I do?"

"You will know when the time comes. Fight your fear, not the one who brings it." Her companions nodded. They all faded.

"Wait!"

Gone. Vivien looked around to see if anyone heard. A woman approached the counter, ignoring her.

Vivien grasped the amulet. She still had no idea how it would help in any confrontation with Mignon. She needed to speak to the Gypsy woman before Sunday.

When they got home, Vivien went for a walk. She worried Lauren would want to go, but her little sister decided to try on her new dress again.

Wearing one of her mother's hand-me-down sweaters, Vivien left the house. Careful not to snag the sweater on the fence, she edged through and climbed the hill. The warmer air made her long for summer and being outside.

The Gypsies received her as usual. The old woman came out of her caravan, and they sat together in the lawn chairs. For several minutes, they didn't speak.

"You are worried. Your friend."

Vivien nodded. "Did you know she would become a problem?"

"How could she not? An undisciplined child who never had a place in the world."

"Do you know how she died?"

"Pneumonia."

The confirmation of the priest's words didn't satisfy Vivien. "There's more to it than that."

"Yes." Another long silence followed. Hester wrapped her shawl tighter around her. "The family who adopted her did not know how to take care of her. She acted wild and reckless, sometimes with so much anger. They thought she was possessed by a demon. They wanted to drive it out."

"You knew her?"

"Yes."

"Did Pere Antoine know her?"

"No, the one before him. He tried to drive the demon away. Mignon ran away, became ill, and died."

"Her adoptive parents buried her in unhallowed ground?"

The woman nodded.

"Under her birth name?"

The woman nodded again. "They wanted no one to know they were her parents."

"Why didn't you tell me all this before?"

"She had been quiet for so long. I hoped she found peace. When I first saw you, I knew she would like you. I felt her yearning. The amulet should have been enough, but she is . . . has waited so long."

"What am I to do? What she wants . . . I can't . . ."

"The gifts are still sealed in the box?"

"Yes."

Vivien now had more information than before, yet she felt there must be more the woman could tell her. Why did she hesitate? Suddenly, she knew.

"You're her grandmother, aren't you?"

Hester looked away. Vivien waited for her to answer.

"Is she your granddaughter? You're trying to protect her, not me."

"Both of you," the woman said without answering the question.

"How? How can you protect both of us?"

CHAPTER

TWENTY-ONE

The church door was unlocked even though Pere Antoine had gone away. He said he never locked it. Vivien hadn't quite believed him. From what he'd said the week before, he left right after morning services to meet with his bishop and wouldn't return until early evening.

A few candles burned in the stand, scenting the air with wax and smoke. Sunlight shone through the stained-glass windows, creating patches of rainbow colors on the floor.

She wandered toward the main altar. The one in the basilica in Saintes was grander, more elaborate. This one seemed uncared for, which she hadn't noticed before. To her mind, the better one sat in the niche. Smaller and simpler, yet with enough religious paraphernalia, it spoke more of devotion and beauty. She went to the stand and lit a candle.

She never prayed and only went to church when Mama insisted. Lauren enjoyed going, or at least she seemed to. Yet, none of them had been to church since leaving Tennessee.

"Religion is about judgement and dividing people," Mignon's voice said behind her.

115

Vivien turned toward her. "Not always. Some people are better for following the rules of a religion."

"I never met anybody like that."

"Was your mother religious?"

Mignon barked a laugh. "The great whore. I don't think so."

"How about your adoptive mother?"

"You've been busy. Who told you about her?"

"No one." The Gypsy woman had only told her that Mignon had been adopted and abandoned, with no details about the woman or her husband.

"She and the priest tried to beat religion into me. They thought a demon possessed me."

"I don't believe in demons."

"You should. They are not easy to identify, though." Mignon ran her hands down the blue fabric of her skirt.

"Do you believe you were possessed?"

"Of course not. Unless you call my mother a demon."

"You remember her?"

"Yours is a wonderful mother, is she not? Caring. Healing your wounds. Listening to your troubles. I bet she is a good cook, too. You would miss her if she was gone." Mignon wandered into the main sanctuary. She stopped and looked around. "It's such a cold place."

"I'm sure it's much warmer when more people are in here."

The ghost went to the altar and leaned against it facing Vivien. She smiled. "Imagine you defending religion."

"Yeah. I guess it's Pere Antoine I'm really defending. He believes and he's a kind man."

"Don't believe the face he shows in public. All priests are zealots who will sacrifice anyone to their prejudices."

It occurred to Vivien that what Mignon said sounded more like an adult argument than one from someone her own age.

Sadness tightened her chest. She genuinely liked Mignon when she was in a softer mood. When they talked about France or the States and people they knew. At that moment, she seemed hard as nails.

I'd better get this over with.

"I have something for you," she said. "Well, I want to return something." She pulled the metal box out of her coat pocket.

"What is it?" Mignon looked up from the box. Her expression changed from curiosity to anger. "I don't want it."

"I'm sorry, but I can't keep them. I'll be gone next year, and I think I should leave them with you."

She held up the metal box wrapped with the silver chain. Mignon stared at it. Without warning, she swept the box out of Vivien's hand onto the floor. It landed on the stone with a bang, which echoed from the walls. The chain skittered across the stone floor, and the lid popped open. Vivien cried out and backed away as maggots squirmed out onto the floor.

"What did you give me?"

Mignon laughed. "They were real as long as you believed."

Vivien spun around and ran to the door. She pulled it open enough to slip through and ran toward home. The air had turned cold, and she stopped to cover nose and mouth with her hands, trying to warm the air she gulped in.

She faced toward home. She doubted Mignon would follow but didn't turn to be sure.

She walked more slowly the rest of the way, stopped short of the gate, and leaned against the stone wall of the derelict building next door. She looked up and down the street. No one in sight.

Why was Mignon here? What could she do for her? The reasons for her earlier experiences—the nurse yearning for her daughter, the Japanese/American girl wanting everyone to know the truth about her death—all became clear in a short time. She'd known Mignon longer than any of them but so far had no clue what to do. How could she help Mignon?

Mignon doesn't want help. She has her own agenda.

Vivien didn't believe herself to be the first one tormented by this unhappy ghost. How long had Mignon been targeting living children? Could she help her stop?

This ghost might be too much for her to deal with alone. But who could help her? Not Mama, who'd made it clear she couldn't interfere. Hester, Mignon's grandmother? Pere Antoine? He would be held back by the church.

She walked slowly, wondering with each step, what she could do. When she reached the gate, she remembered the silver cross and chain. The Gypsy woman wanted them back.

TWENTY-TWO

"Concentrate, Vivien." Madame Guilbeau scolded in frustration.

Vivien had become so focused on the problem with Mignon, she had trouble thinking about anything else. Mr. Gregersen noticed Monday, and she tried harder to pay better attention in class. Today, Tuesday, went well until morning recess. By the time Madame Guilbeau appeared for their session, Vivien's mind kept wandering.

"I'm sorry," Vivien said.

"There is a problem?"

"Sort of. I'm not sure what to do."

"Perhaps I could help."

"I'm not sure. No, I don't think so." If only someone could. The French teacher studied her pupil until Vivien became uncomfortable.

"You have encountered someone or something?"

"Yes, but . . ."

"Might it be . . ." The teacher turned to stare at the other students playing all sorts of games. Vivien followed her gaze.

They all seemed so happy, laughing and yelling, running around or jumping rope. Two boys threw a baseball back and forth. "Might it be you have met someone, and it has become uncomfortable?"

"In a way."

"If it is not a boy, it might be a girl."

"How would you know it's not a boy?"

"I have lived here a very long time. There are stories, ever since the war."

"What kind of stories?"

"A woman in La Rochelle during the first World War. A prostitute with the name Solange Cuvier. She had a daughter, father not known."

"After the girl was born, her mother sent her to an orphanage in this area," Vivien said.

"Ah, you have heard of her."

"Not the whole story. I heard that a couple in the village adopted her, but they couldn't control her."

"*Oui.* Some say they did not try very hard, but the mother and priest in the church there tried to help her. In the end she died, it is said due to what the priest and mother did. Several years after that, children in the area began dying at about the same age, eleven to twelve. No one knew why. Always pretty ones who kept to themselves. Shy but smart."

"When did the last one die?"

"Three years ago, I think. Some people believed the Cuvier girl finally found peace."

"Do they know what she did or why she did it?"

"No one knows for certain. Each child died from a different cause. It is said the dead girl was lonely and wanted friends. Maybe, maybe not."

Vivien heard some of the story from Pere Antoine, which she thought made it true. The rest Mignon hinted at herself.

She'd said she wanted Vivien to be with her forever. Only one way to do that.

The bell rang, and Madame Guilbeau stood. "Be careful, *ma petite*. If this girl wants you . . ." She shrugged. "I wish I could help."

Vivien thanked her for the information and for caring. They went back inside. Vivien gave her full attention to Mr. Gregersen and her schoolwork.

That evening, she sat at the kitchen table, writing down what she knew about her friend. She found it very surprising that so many people knew something about the ghost, all from slightly different angles.

The woman ghost in the department store. What role did she play? The children standing behind her. How many? Six, eight? What did they have to do with Mignon?

Vivien shivered. Had they each been Mignon's special friend?

Mignon didn't appear for the rest of the week. Vivien wanted to believe she'd given up on her but couldn't quite. She kept to her usual routine at recess and taking walks in the evenings. The days had gotten longer. Forsythia bloomed against the fences in the school yard, the yellow flowers adding brightness to the sunny days.

When she went to the church on Sunday, Pere Antoine greeted her. "*Bonjour*, Vivien. *Ça va?*"

"*Ça va.* I'm surprised to see you."

"Ah, I must go to St. Jean, so now I do my chores. I will return by *cinq heures*."

"Have a safe trip."

"*Merci.* I will see you next Sunday."

Vivien laughed. "Probably."

Visiting the church each Sunday had become so much a part of her routine that she couldn't imagine not being there. It was the most peaceful moment she had all week until Mignon showed up.

She helped the priest straighten up the pews and check the candles. "Father, did you find a silver cross on a silver chain in here this week?"

"*Non*. Did you lose one?"

"Yes, but I'm not sure where."

Mignon must have whisked it away, although she'd expected the silver chain to have some sort of resistance to her ghostly powers.

Pere Antoine promised to keep an eye out for it while he finished the chores. He thanked her for helping and left. Vivien went into the niche and sat in one of the chairs, looking at the small altar. Someone had added two small vases with lavender blossoms. Their fragrance surrounded her. She rose and lit the candles with a match from a small box almost hidden behind the candlesticks.

She returned to the chair and resumed waiting for Mignon to appear. After another half an hour, she decided the ghost would not come today. Where was she and what was she doing?

When Vivien got home, she went into the bedroom to find her book. Lauren's diary lay open on the bed. Feeling only a little guilty, she picked it up. Nearly twenty pages had been filled with her sister's cramped writing. She carried it to the window to get more light and went back two days' entries.

What fun it's been to learn French from my new friend. She's so much bettr than Mrs. Biul-beau with her conjugtions.

Vivien shook her head at the misspellings. But she froze

when she read the next line.

> *Mignon is so pretty and has such pretty cloths. I wish I could spend more tim with her but she says we have to be carefull. Viviene might not like it if she finds out.*

Vivien turned to the last entry.

> *Mignon wants to meet in the old house where she used to live. It's real close to ours. I'll tell mama I'm going to Estelle's so she won't worry.*

Had Mignon given up on her and turned her sights to Lauren? Her little sister was three years younger. Did she think Lauren would be easier to convince? Or did she threaten Lauren as a way to make Vivien give in? If only Lauren couldn't see the ghosts, as she had that time in Breckinridge, although it seemed to be that the ghosts let her see them.

She read the words again. A house near theirs. Where? Across the street? Next door? She grabbed her coat off the hook beside the door and ran out. Mama called her name, but she didn't stop.

Empty lots on both sides of their house. Then, a repair shop to the north. To the south, an empty building that might have been lived in. Across the street, on the corner, a small house. It had not been occupied since they moved in.

She closed her eyes and took hold of the amulet in her fist. Which one? She opened her eyes and went across the street and tried the front door. Locked. A back door? Yes.

It stood slightly ajar. Cooler air seeped through the crack.

Slowly, she pushed the door. The hinges squealed and she stopped. She stepped through sideways, and the hinges made no more noise.

Inside, the house looked more derelict than the outside. The tiny kitchen in which she found herself had a large sink set in a wooden frame. A table, the veneer peeling, sat against the wall to her right. Debris covered the floor. No one had lived there for many years.

The floorboards creaked with each step. At the door into the living room, she stopped and peeked around the door frame. The living room had two old easy chairs with stuffing showing through holes in the fabric. More debris lay scattered on the floor. Two more doors to the right, both closed.

A soft sound came from one of the other rooms. Vivien tiptoed across the living room. She put her ear against the door on the left. Nothing. When she listened at the one on the right, the sounds came again.

Slowly she turned the doorknob. She threw the door open and took one step inside. Several pieces of wooden furniture from the other rooms had been stacked along the walls. In the center of the room, two girls sat on a blanket spread on the floor holding hands. They looked up at Vivien, eyes wide.

"Vivien!" Lauren cried.

"Are you all right?"

"Sure. We were just talking."

"About what?"

"She's alone and likes to have someone to talk to."

"We have become friends," Mignon said. "Your little sister is so kind to me."

"It's time to get home," Vivien said to Lauren. She kept her eyes on Mignon. "Mama wants us."

"I told her I was at Estelle's. Don't tell her, please."

"Don't tell her you lied?"

Lauren nodded.

"We'll talk about it when we get home." Vivien gave her sister a hand up. "Here," she said and handed her the coat.

Lauren walked toward the door.

"Come see me again," Mignon said.

"I will." Lauren stopped to look back, but Vivien gave her a little push. "Bye."

"Vivien." Mignon got to her feet.

"Go home, Lauren. I'll be right there." Vivien faced the ghost.

"You or her. It makes no difference to me."

"You won't have either of us. From what I've been hearing, you have plenty of others to keep you company."

"They get so tiresome. Nothing new in their world."

"It's your world, too."

"Yes."

"Our world is here and now." She touched the amulet with cold fingertips.

"That will not help you."

"We'll see. If it won't, I'll find something that will."

Mignon laughed and faded. "We'll see." The words echoed her own.

That night, as the sisters lay in bed, Vivien said, "Please don't ever see Mignon again."

"I like her. I know she used to be your friend, but she's my friend now."

"No, Lauren. She's no one's friend. She's a ghost who means us harm."

"No, she isn't. I touched her. She's real. You're just jealous." Lauren turned her back to her sister.

Vivien lay awake a long time. Was she jealous of Lauren's friendship with Mignon? True or not, Lauren must not see the ghost again. How to keep it from happening?

TWENTY-THREE

Monday came and Vivien begged off from going to school, saying she had a stomachache. Before Lauren caught the bus, she told her sister that she wouldn't tell Mama about the lie, as long as she stayed away from Mignon. Lauren agreed and left in a pout.

Vivien lay propped up in bed, a book in her lap. She pretended to read. Instead, ideas of how to get Mignon out of her life came and went.

Mignon didn't have a problem to solve like Nurse Armstrong in Breckinridge or Yoshi Narita in Manchester. On the ship, the female ghost and the male ghost had been locked in a battle over the safety of children moving from and to the States with their fathers on military orders. Like Mignon, that male ghost was the problem, not one looking for a solution. She'd drained all of the energy from him on the ship through physical contact.

She didn't think the same tactic would work on Mignon. The strength of the girl's energy might be more than Vivien could handle, even with the help of the amulet. Not that it had been of much help so far.

Why did the old Gypsy woman give it to her?

Vivien believed it held properties of protection. Maybe it had provided the strength to resist Mignon's temptations so far. With Mignon's sights now on Lauren, Vivien couldn't wait any longer to find a resolution.

Once more, she considered who might help. The Gypsy was Mignon's grandmother, so her loyalties might be divided. Pere Antoine may suspect something had happened, but would he be able to accept the existence of a ghost? Madame Guilbeau knew of the stories that might center around Mignon's desire for the company of more and more children, but she could hardly ask her for help. Her talking about the stories didn't mean she believed them.

Sadly, Mama might know all about such a situation, but she could not interfere. She couldn't for some mysterious reason.

Nurse Armstrong targeted Vivien in their first encounter, almost as Mignon had. They wanted her to join them in death. In Mignon's case, however, she had already gathered several other children to be her friends. Never enough. She always needed one more.

If the so-called friends she already had become boring, why did she keep them from going on to their rest?

Their energy!

She used their energy. Added to her own, they made Mignon stronger than she could be alone. If she could free the others, send them on their way, Mignon might weaken, just like the ghost on the ship. He had accumulated energy from the children he preyed on, and sent them back to their parents, weak and possibly dying. Mignon collected their spirits to feed off their energy.

Separating Mignon from the children would weaken her, make her more vulnerable. But how? She only saw the others at the department store. She could ask Mama to take her there, but too many people, too many questions. She needed to go alone. Too far to walk. Who else could take her?

Her best hope was the Gypsy woman.

The clock in the living room cuckooed three times. Later than she expected. She threw back the covers and got out of bed. Mama came in while she dressed.

"I thought you were sick."

"Sorry, Mama. I have to go see Hester."

"Because of the ghost?"

Vivien nodded. At the door, she slipped her feet into the short boots and knelt down to tie them. "I need to be gone a while. If the woman will take me where I need to go. Can you think of something to tell Daddy?" She took her coat off the hook in the hall near the door.

"I guess you'll be spending the night with a friend."

Vivien smiled. "Sounds right."

Frightened in spite of her determination, Vivien hugged her mother. She opened the door and stepped onto the stoop. Temperatures had fluctuated the past few days from almost warm to cold. Spring kept trying to break the hold of winter. Today the cold held.

When she reached the Gypsy camp, Angelette went into the woman's caravan to let her know. The old woman came out and gave Vivien a smile. Too tense to smile or sit in the usual lawn chair, Vivien nodded. The woman frowned.

"Something has happened?"

"Mignon threatened my sister yesterday. It's time to do something."

"What will you do?"

"I need you or someone to take me to the department store in St. Jean. The other children are there."

"How do you know?"

"I've seen them."

"All of them?"

"All of her friends. I haven't seen Mignon there."

"What can you do?"

"I don't know for sure. I have an idea. I need to get into the store so I can be there after they close."

The woman sat down. From her expression, Vivien suspected she was undecided about helping.

"Do you want to help? Or do you want to protect Mignon?"

"There are many ways to protect her."

"Shouldn't she be at peace? She's a threat to the life of any kid who might be unlucky enough to see her. I won't let her take my sister." Instinctively, she didn't say Lauren's name. "Why do you protect Mignon?"

The woman stared at her. "She's unhappy. She craves friends so badly."

"She needs to be put to rest. Help me."

The woman nodded and got to her feet. "Paolo." A man about her daddy's age looked up and walked toward Vivien and the woman. She motioned toward Vivien. "Please to take her to St.-Jean-d'Angély, to the department store."

"Now?"

"Yes."

He frowned. "It's important?" He seemed reluctant. Was he leery of being around her, or did he not want to drive into town?

"Yes, it is," Vivien said.

He nodded and motioned for her to follow him. Vivien leaned over and kissed the woman's cheek. "It's for the best."

"Don't forget the amulet," she said. "Grip it tightly. You'll know when."

The woman sat back down and watched them get in the old pickup and drive away. The truck had no suspension or heat. It also had one speed: slow. Paolo pulled to the curb with half an hour to spare. Vivien thanked him and got out. She waved when he drove away but didn't think he saw her.

Most customers were gone, and the staff moved around in the store getting ready to close. Vivien wandered for a few minutes, nearing the jewelry counter. No one in that part of the store. Pretending to look into the glass cases, she watched to be sure no one would see her slip into the stockroom behind the counters. She felt her way among the shelves and crouched among them. The only light came through the windows in the swinging doors between there and the store.

The few minutes seemed to stretch into an hour, but eventually the lights went out. Vivien waited half an hour to be certain no one remained.

TWENTY-FOUR

Ever so slowly, Vivien made her way to the door. She raised up on tiptoe to see through the window, but it was too high. The door swung outward silently, and she watched for any movement. The only sound, a buzzing she'd never noticed before.

Still on tiptoe, she crept to the jewelry counters. Now what? Would the woman appear? The children?

"Are you here? Please, let me see you."

"I'm here." The woman slowly took shape. "What do you want?"

"The children. Where are they?"

They appeared like a gathering fog. They wavered in and out of view, making it difficult to count, taking form behind the woman.

"These are Mignon's friends."

"*Oui*," the woman said.

"You take care of them."

"*Oui*."

"Why?"

"Mignon asked me to."

"And you do what she asks?" The woman smiled. "What hold does she have on you?" She continued to smile. "Who is Mignon to you?"

"She's such a beautiful girl. Everyone loves her."

The truth came to Vivien. "You're her mother."

"Of course."

"Can you release the children from this world?"

"No. Mignon treasures them."

"But you could if Mignon no longer wanted them."

Vivien took a deep breath and took hold of the amulet. She walked toward the woman, then through her. The children watched her approach with curiosity and no fear. She reached out to a child in the front of the group. One of only two boys, he had a pretty face and blond hair like Mignon's.

Although she could see through him as if he were made of smoke, her hand touched a solid shoulder. He looked at her hand then raised his eyes to her. Nothing showed in those eyes. She reached her free arm around his shoulders and pulled him to her.

"No." The woman moved to stop her but couldn't get close. She reached out but couldn't quite reach.

"Go," Vivien said. "Rest." After a long moment, he slipped away, and her arm fell to her side.

"What are you doing?" the woman asked.

"Setting them free." Vivien felt tired, but her hold on the amulet didn't relax. The stones warmed in her hand. She reached for the nearest girl.

The woman screeched and clawed at her but couldn't reach her. It might be the power of the amulet. Vivien didn't know. With each child she freed, Mignon's mother wailed and threatened. When finished, eight young souls had been freed. The woman had shrunk as if almost everything had been sucked out of her.

"Mignon will avenge me." She sobbed and still tried to reach Vivien.

"She knows where I'll be." Reaching her hand out, Vivien touched the woman's arm then her hand. She held onto it while the woman sobbed. "Rest."

Vivien leaned against the counter and caught her breath. When she felt some strength return, she shuffled out of the jewelry department into the furniture department. She collapsed onto an overstuffed chair similar to the one at home. She curled up and wondered how she would get home.

TWENTY-FIVE

Voices woke her. Sleep had eased her exhaustion, but her mind was fuzzy. In a moment she remembered where she was. The store hadn't opened yet, and she had to hide. She slipped under a dining table, and no one saw her. When the doors were unlocked and people started coming in, she got up and walked out the door.

She stood on the sidewalk, unsure what to do. She'd never noticed if St. Jean had taxis. Even if they did, she had no way to call one nor any money to pay for it.

She turned to the right, thinking it better to keep moving. A horn honked and Paolo's pickup pulled up to the curb. She got in.

"Thanks, Paolo." How did Hester know to send him this morning?

Neither said another word all the way to Asnieres. He stopped in front of her house, and she climbed out. Vivien waved when he pulled away. For now, she needed a proper rest.

Mama came into the hall when the door closed. "You look exhausted."

"I am."

Mama helped her undress and get into bed. She woke in the early afternoon before Daddy or Lauren got home. Mama fixed scrambled eggs and toast, and Vivien devoured every crumb. Afterward, she needed to think and went out to the back yard to sit on the well wall.

What happened with the ghosts was beyond her understanding. She'd taken their energy and still felt exhausted when they disappeared. When she took the energy of the soldier on the ship, it gave her a feeling of euphoria. Her seasickness disappeared. So much strength. Not this time. She couldn't figure out why.

Daddy called to tell Mama he would be home late and not to hold dinner for him. Although he knew nothing about the ghosts and Vivien's abilities, his presence always gave her a feeling of calm and strength outside of herself that could be relied on. She'd looked forward to his being at home tonight.

She and Mama made spaghetti for dinner, expecting Lauren to get home from school soon. And they waited. Half an hour past the time Mama worried, and Vivien suspected. Once more she wrapped up to go out.

"I'll find her," she said.

With the sun beginning to set, the air grew cooler. Vivien ran across the street to the back door of the old house. Empty and dark inside. She ran down the block to the church. The door stood ajar. She stopped and took a deep breath, taking hold of the amulet. The protective stones thrummed against her hand. All of the strength of the children had gone into the amulet and now flowed into her.

She pushed the door open, and her footsteps echoed from the stone walls. Sunlight had faded and she could see little. A dark figure struck a match and lit candles on the altar. Mignon turned and blew out the match, a smile on her lips. To the left, Pere Antoine slumped on one of the pews facing away from the door. His head turned side to side as if in denial. Lauren lay at the ghost's feet, her eyes rolled back in her head, her mouth slack. Mignon reached down and grabbed Vivien's sister by the arm and pulled her to her feet. The paleness of her skin made her as ghostlike as Mignon. She would have fallen to the floor if Mignon hadn't held her up.

"I see you now have the strength to light the candles," Vivien said.

"A lot of good it did you to take the others away from me."

"How did you know?"

"Know you got your energy from them? I've seen it before." Again, Vivien saw the soldier on the ship in her mind's eye struggling to get away from her. She realized the energy from the ghost children had flowed into the amulet instead of directly into her. Until she needed it.

"And your mother."

Mignon's howl echoed from the stone walls. "Her punishment is over, thanks to you. But she spent time in hell helping me."

"She's at peace now."

"She will never have peace. She doesn't deserve it."

Vivien looked to her sister. "Lauren, are you all right?"

Her sister tried to raise her head and focus, but Mignon pulled her closer.

"She's mine now. You could have saved her, but you wouldn't make the sacrifice."

"She'll never be yours."

"Look at her. She's nearly gone. Another few minutes, and all of her life energy will be gone."

Vivien took three steps forward, keeping her gaze on her best friend. Mignon dug her fingers into Lauren's arm.

"Stop! I can make it painful."

"Leave her. I'll go with you."

"It is too late. I wanted you, my best friend. You were more than the others. More than your little sister. We could have had years together."

"I didn't want years with you. But I'll go with you now."

"Will you promise? Will you come to me without a struggle?"

"Yes. I promise."

Mignon dropped the spent match and reached out to Vivien. "Come then."

"Let her go."

"When I have a hold on you."

Vivien walked to her and held out her hand.

Mignon took it in hers. She laughed. "Now I have you both."

Vivien reached toward Lauren and pushed, trying to free her from Mignon's grasp. Mignon struggled to keep her hold on both of them. Vivien jerked the amulet hard, breaking the catch, and slapped it against Mignon's breast. She held tightly to the ghost's hand and raised her leg, pressing her foot against Lauren's side. She was losing her balance and pressed against her sister harder. Mignon's hold on Lauren broke and she stumbled to the nearest pew and slumped onto it.

Mignon tried to back away from the pressure of the amulet, but Vivien wrapped her other arm around her friend and pulled her close. Energy within like the stones flowed through her while it sucked energy from Mignon. The children's faces flashed through her mind. Vivien pushed Mignon against the altar and hugged her tightly.

The ghost choked and gasped. "I loved you." The words were barely audible.

"I know. I loved you, too."

Mignon slipped to the floor, and Vivien knelt to keep her arms around her. Mignon's eyes closed and with a sigh, she faded away.

Vivien sat on the floor, tears streaming down her face. She had loved Mignon, her one and only best friend.

"Vivien."

She wiped at the tears with her hand and looked over to see Lauren trying to get to her feet. She crawled to her little sister on all fours and put her hand on her shoulder. "Rest a moment." She kissed her sister's forehead. "How do you feel?"

"Very tired."

"Do you remember what happened?"

"Yeah. Mignon met the bus and asked me to walk to the church with her. This is the church?" She looked around. "Anyway, we sat down, and she began talking. A priest walked in, and she got mad."

"That's it?"

"Yeah. Where is she?"

"She's gone."

"Oh."

Vivien struggled to her feet and went to Pere Antoine. She pushed his head back so she could see his face. His eyes were closed as if he slept.

"Pere Antoine." She said his name twice more, but he didn't react.

She held the amulet against his chest and the stones warmed. The priest's eyes blinked a few times and opened. "You're okay?" she said.

"What . . ."

She sat down beside him and watched the flames of the

candles flickering on the altar. Pere Antoine sat up and rubbed his eyes. Lauren sneezed.

No one spoke for a while. Vivien hoped the two would forget everything that happened, which appeared to be a good bet. She stood unsteadily and held onto the back of the pew.

"Is she gone?" the priest asked.

"Yes, she's gone."

"It was the ghost of Mignon Cuvier?"

"Yes."

"Are you all right?"

Vivien nodded.

"Bless you, my child," the priest said.

She nodded thanks and went over to help Lauren to her feet. Energy flowed through her into her sister. It was nearly dark when they walked home, arm in arm.

TWENTY-SIX

Vivien trudged up the hill once more. When she arrived in the camp, Angelette went inside the caravan as usual, but it took longer for the woman to appear. Vivien sat in the lawn chair and took a deep breath.

She still felt tired. Lauren had no memory of what happened to her, for which Vivien was grateful. Pere Antoine never asked about what happened, so he might not remember, either, but she wasn't so sure about him.

A potted geranium sitting beside the caravan steps bloomed bright coral in the spring sunlight. She raised her head for the sun to shine on her face. The sound of the woman on the steps sounded slower than usual.

Vivien opened her eyes and sat up in the chair. The woman stopped beside her and looked down.

"She's gone." The woman's voice quavered.

"As far as I know. Time will tell."

The woman nodded and sat down. "She wasn't evil."

"No, just lonely."

"The others?"

"Her mother and the other children? They're at peace now, too."

"Her mother helped her." The old Gypsy shook her head. "Guilty conscience."

They sat quietly as if listening. "How did you know?" the woman asked.

"About her mother?"

"Her and me."

"How hard it was for you to help me against Mignon. And her mother. Mignon once described her to me. Especially the clothes."

The woman nodded.

For the first time since confronting Mignon, Vivien relaxed. The warmth of the sun made her sleepy. She wanted to say more to the old woman, grandmother of the girl who nearly took her life, but she couldn't remember all the things she'd thought to say.

She pulled the cross on the chain from her coat pocket and held them out to the woman. "I nearly lost them." Pere Antoine had found them after all the excitement and guessed they were Vivien's. He'd promptly forgotten them until a few days later. "The box is gone I'm afraid."

The woman took them and wrapped the chain around her hand. Vivien touched the amulet. "Do you want this back."

"No. You will need it."

I hope not.

She wrapped the cord around the stones and put it in the pocket of her coat. "Thank you."

The woman nodded. Tears shone in her eyes. Vivien wanted to feel sorry for her losing both daughter and grand-daughter for the second time but couldn't manage it. She'd almost taken Mignon's side, leaving Vivien on her own. She'd given her the amulet but did not tell her how to use it. Nor did she say anything about what she would face.

"You do not know why you have this curse?" The old woman looked straight ahead.

"No, none of us do."

"Your first ancestor to set foot in America had a son. He was born there. He grew up and as a young man, he fell in love with a young woman servant. He promised to marry her, but his parents judged the girl to be unsuitable. They found another girl from a wealthy family, and he married her.

"The woman he loved was with child. She raised a fuss and his family had her charged with some offense. She was flogged and the baby was born. She never fully recovered from the beating and on her deathbed she cursed the son's wife and the daughters she would bear. His wife lost her mind after giving birth to two daughters. She screamed about seeing ghosts hovering over her as the second was born."

Vivien's heart beat wildly and she gasped for breath. She sat with her hand on her breast, willing her heart to slow down.

"How do you know all of this?" Vivien asked.

The woman turned and looked at her with a sad smile. "I am a Roma."

"Will this curse ever end?"

The woman shrugged.

Vivien closed her eyes and took a deep breath. "Will you be leaving soon? Gypsies don't hang around very long."

"Roma. We call ourselves Roma."

"Not Gypsies?"

"Never."

"I'll remember."

She walked back down the hill, hoping to never have to take this walk again.

She heard Daddy's voice in the living room when she closed the door behind her. Mama called, "Supper's ready." Vivien hung up her coat on the hook and slipped off the boots. When she went into the kitchen, Daddy gave her a big hug, which surprised her. They sat down at the table, and she looked at Mama for an explanation. Mama avoided looking at her.

EPILOGUE

AUGUST 23, 1959

Large airplanes lifted into the air across the field from the terminal. In another hour, Vivien and her family would board a Military Air Transport Service, or MATS, plane and fly from Paris to New York City. She felt both excitement and a little nervous at her very first flight.

At least they weren't taking a ship back. After the trip to Europe, she hoped to stay away from ships for a long time.

Three days ago, they'd taken a train from St. Jean to Paris and then a cab to a hotel. They couldn't afford a great deal of sightseeing except to wander around the city. Not far from the hotel, they found a used bookstore. The rest of the family left her there and wandered farther. She was to meet them back at the hotel in no more than an hour.

~

THE SMELL of the bookstore and the shelves of old books brought memories of the store in Saintes and buying the Jules Verne novel. Of Mignon helping her with the correct French words. Of their walking together back to the bus. Tears made it hard to read the book titles but she sniffed them back. Several books about France caught her eye, but Daddy wouldn't be happy if she bought even one since they'd have to carry it with them.

She was about to leave when she noticed a small volume on the Palace of Versailles. At the end of the eighth grade, she'd graduated as valedictorian. With only three in her class, it didn't seem like such an achievement. Mama and Daddy were proud, though. Their graduation trip was to Paris, so she'd seen much more of the city over that long weekend. She'd seen the view from the top of the Eiffel Tower. They had lunch at the American Embassy. The mirrors were dirty in the Hall of Mirrors, where peace treaties had been signed. The guide who led them through the Palace at Versailles took a shine to her and gave her a small flower he plucked in the garden while telling them a romantic story.

She was surprised by the appearance of another ghost, a young woman, who took her on a short tour of other rooms, closed to the public.

It was her strangest experience so far. The ghost, dressed in 18th century clothes, seemed to want company and to display her knowledge of the palace and the events that happened there. No other agenda. Vivien learned so much more than was included in the official tour. She wanted the book as a reminder of what she saw and learned. It wasn't expensive and she convinced herself it would fit into the bag she would carry onto the plane, which was scheduled to leave tomorrow morning.

After they landed in New York City, they would pick up their car and drive to Tennessee to stay with Grandma for several days. From there, they would drive to Ft. Hood, Texas,

Daddy's next posting. None of them knew much about Texas, but they'd learn.

Just as she'd learned much about France and come to love living there. Over the two years, she'd visited the Chateau du Roche Courbons, eaten her first oyster in La Rochelle, seen German submarine pens in that same city, and walked on the beach at Royan. She'd visited Paris three times. She spoke passable French.

Would any of this experience mean a thing in Texas? She suspected she'd still be an outsider.

"FLIGHT 734 IS NOW ready for boarding. All passengers, please have your tickets ready. Flight 734 ready for boarding."

No. I don't want to go.

Living in France had become a great adventure, one that for her hadn't entirely ended. Still, so many things she hadn't done, so many places she hadn't seen. Would she ever come back?

Mama appeared behind her and put her hand on Vivien's shoulder. She turned and hugged her mother with tears in her eyes.

"It's time."

"I know."

"You'll come back someday."

They walked together toward the gate to join Daddy and Lauren.

This will be another adventure. Without ghosts, I hope.

The woman at the gate took her ticket and smiled.

ABOUT THE AUTHOR

Cary Herwig is an author of middle grade/young adult horror fiction. This is the second book in *The Army Brat Hauntings* series and Cary's thirteenth published book.

You can find Cary's blog at https://caryosbornewriter.blogspot.com/ and email her at iroshiok@gmail.com.

ALSO BY CARY HERWIG

The Army Brat Hauntings

The Ghost's Daughter

The World Ends at the River

Friends Like Dust